*"**The Zoo Animals' Faraway Dream** is a touching, beautifully written story with a heart-warming cast of zoo characters. The story makes you laugh and sigh, while also urging you to stop and think about the plight of many zoo animals in our world."*
~ Sonia Faruqi, author of Project Animal Farm (an award-winning investigation of the truth behind factory farming) and The Oyster Thief (an underwater odyssey)

Also by Kathryn Rose Newey

Animals in the Forest:
The Day Terrible Things Came
(A story to save the Earth)

Ilnoblet Elmer and the Alien Water Thieves

Visit the author's website at
KathrynRoseNewey.com

Dedication

To all animals on Earth who are imprisoned in cages, enclosures, laboratories, stalls, pens, crates, pools and tanks. May humans see, one day set you free, and let you be. Love and strength.

Acknowledgements

To those human beings who feel the suffering of caged animals, who try to ease it or work for animals' freedom, and who educate other humans about this shameful and cruel issue ~ your actions are noticed, appreciated and inspiring. Thank you.

To those family members and friends who laboriously and tirelessly read through each new draft of my manuscripts and make useful comments each time ~ you write with me. Thank you.

The Zoo Animals' Faraway Dream

Special Edition with Bonus Chapter

A Story to Save Caged Animals

Kathryn Rose Newey

The Zoo Animals' Faraway Dream

Special Edition [Edition 2.1] with Bonus Chapter.
ISBN-13: 978-1-78926-498-2 (paperback, 2nd edition)
ISBN-13: 978-1-78926-499-9 (eBook, 2nd edition)

Copyright © 2019 by Kathryn Rose Newey
All rights reserved.

No parts of this publication may be reproduced, stored in a retrieval system, or transmitted in any form or by any means, electronic, mechanical, photocopying, recording, or otherwise, without the prior written permission of the copyright owner.

This book is sold subject to the condition that it shall not, by way of trade or otherwise, be lent, resold, hired out, or otherwise circulated without the copyright holder's prior consent in any form of binding or cover other than that in which it is published and without a similar condition including this condition being imposed on the subsequent purchaser. Under no circumstances may any part of this book be photocopied for resale.

This is a work of fiction. Any similarity between the characters and situations within its pages and places or persons, living or dead, is unintentional and coincidental.

Cover Photograph: Claudia Paulussen/Shutterstock.com

Publisher Imprint: KathrynRoseNewey.com / Independent Publishing Network

THE ZOO ANIMALS' FARAWAY DREAM

CONTENTS

Also by Kathryn Rose Newey 1

Dedication 2

Acknowledgements 2

PART ONE ~ A STORY WITH TWO ENDINGS 9

1 – The Little Zoo 11

2 – A Bit Rusty 19

3 – Being Natural 30

4 – Deliriously Happy 40

5 – A Visitor 48

6 – Sweet Redemption 57

7 – The Faraway Dream 66

8 – The Faraway Nightmare 75

9 – A Terrible Thing 85

10 – Being Free 94

11 – A True Leader 106

12 – Separation Anxiety 116

13 – Fat in the Fire 125

14 – Pig in a Poke 136

15 – Calm Before the Storm 145

16 – A Moment of Truth 155

17 – Floods of Tears 164

18 – Still Waters Run Deep (Ending One) 173

18 – Still Waters Run Deep (Ending Two) 183

THE ZOO ANIMALS' FARAWAY DREAM

PART TWO ~ THE TRUTH 195

19 – About Caged Animals 197

Facts about caged and confined animals 198

20 – About Zoos 204

History of zoos 204

If zoos aren't good, why do we have them? 207

Zoos: the whole truth 210

Shouldn't we let all caged animals go free? 212

21 – How Can You Help? 215

22 – More Things to Know 220

About the Author 231

KATHRYN ROSE NEWEY

THE ZOO ANIMALS' FARAWAY DREAM

PART ONE ~ A STORY WITH TWO ENDINGS

KATHRYN ROSE NEWEY

1 – *The Little Zoo*

It was sunny, for once, in the little zoo. The animal inhabitants woke to a few rays of sunshine cautiously trickling into their cages, creeping over their food bowls, playing hide and seek between their cage bars, and reaching warming fingers onto their cold fur or feathers.

Or at least the lucky ones did: those animals whose cages faced the morning sunshine.

The rest, whose cages faced in other directions, shivered against their concrete floors and sandy pits, and strained against their bars or walls, in the hope that a lone ray of sunshine might take pity on them and warm them, even if only temporarily.

But the sunshine didn't last long. The clouds, never happy to let the sun simply shine and warm up the animals' hearts and bones, bustled and jostled across the sky, and soon it was grey and dull, and the sky seemed to close in and press down on the imprisoned souls again.

~~~~~~~~~~~~~~~~~~~~~~~~~~~~

But those few moments of warmth and light were enough to cheer up Shiro the mongoose.

'It's definitely going to be a good day today', she thought, watching the sun rays reach warily across her enclosure. Even as they slithered away, and the domineering clouds took over, she was determined that it wouldn't ruin anything.

Shiro, perhaps due to some misguided maternal instincts, felt it was her duty to be positive and forceful in this little zoo; the other animals needed her guidance! Sometimes she had to insist they be happy, or at least try to be.

Every morning, in her busy-body way, she rounded up all the other mongooses – she clapped her paws quickly to catch the attention of the little ones playing, and called sharply to the sleepy adults lurking in their holes – then marched them all up to the food bowls at the front of the mongoose enclosure, where they waited for the human workers to give them hastily-prepared and measly portions of food.

Serving breakfast was always one of the first activities undertaken by the human workers – those strange, large and noisy creatures who appeared to roam freely outside the cages, who brought the animals food and water, and who occasionally cleaned out the cages.

The mongoose enclosure was quite spacious, compared to some other animal enclosures. It had concrete walls which followed a roughly oval shape, with a loose pile of rocks and sand in the middle. The pile was now slightly sunken and fallen down, but was nevertheless just far away enough from the tops of the walls in every direction, so that no mongoose, perhaps intent on escape, might succeed in its endeavours.

Shiro, one of the mongooses who had been there the longest, could still remember a time when Mungo, an older and rather grumpy mongoose, had decided one day that he was leaving. Simply leaving. He didn't say where to.

As you may know, mongooses do possess the skills of digging. But the human designers of their enclosure must have known this, and had installed wire and concrete edges to the walls deep enough into the ground, just that bit too far for the mongooses to dig under and escape to freedom. Some of the mongooses had tried, of course, but to no avail. So Mungo had decided the only way out was over the tops of the mongoose enclosure walls.

No amount of arguing or pleading with him could sway his plan. Shiro, as was her way, tried to assert her authority and forbade him to do so. She was worried that his bid for freedom might catch on with the other mongooses, or perhaps even some of the other zoo animals, and that simply wouldn't do. After all, the zoo was a happy place and needed to remain that way, with as little disorder as was animally possible.

Besides, none of the mongooses knew what lay beyond the zoo. They didn't even know the full extent of the little zoo itself. They had tried to argue with Mungo that if he were to go, no humans would bring him food, and then how would he eat? Also, they couldn't be completely sure, but when they had been able to look out, from the top of the rocky pile in their enclosure, none of the mongooses had seen any mongoose burrows of hollows or other safe places for him to sleep in. And again, it couldn't be fully confirmed, but they didn't think that any human workers would come and clean his living space, if he were to live out there.

But Mungo was beyond listening to anyone. He had climbed to the top of the rock pile in the centre of the enclosure, and stretched his paws and body as far as he could towards the nearest wall. Then he had tried to leap at the wall a few times, but had kept falling down before he got anywhere close.

He had simply climbed up and tried again. He had repeated this perhaps ten times, and was getting tired and dusty from all his falls in the dirt, when one of the humans who worked at the zoo had come up and shouted, banging their hands on the walls.

Mungo, as well as all the other mongooses, who had all been lined up watching him, fled into their sandy holes under the rocks in terror.

Mungo had never got the opportunity to try and escape again. He had fallen asleep that evening and never woken up.

It had taken three days and three nights before the human workers had even realized. Then they'd unceremoniously tossed his little stiffened body onto a pile of dirty straw in a nearby wheelbarrow, and wheeled him away, all the while talking and whistling.

~~~~~~~~~~~~~~~~~~~~~~~~~~~~

2 – A Bit Rusty

Across from the mongoose enclosure, and only visible to the mongooses through the bars of another cage, was a cylindrical cage with close bars and criss-crossed wire covering the bars, as if to make doubly sure that no small creatures would be able to force themselves out.

This meant that the single occupant, Kolobe the

warthog, could unfortunately not thrust his nose or little warthog tusks out of his bars, try as he might. He had to be content with being constrained within his wired and barred cage, which at least allowed him to see out, if nothing else.

His cage, being round, cylindrical and with closer bars, appeared to the human visitors more like an oversized, ornamental birdcage than something to accommodate a warthog.

Indeed the warthog's cage had once housed pigeons; but that was a long time ago. The only zoo animal old enough to remember this was Ndlovu the elephant, whose enclosure was next door.

The elephant enclosure, more of a pit, was the largest in the little zoo, as one might hope and expect, since she was the largest animal in the zoo. Sadly Ndlovu didn't get to see much of the goings-on in the zoo, because her sandy – often muddy - and once grassy enclosure was purposefully sunken far below the ground level of the rest of the zoo, and had high and thick, elephant-proof walls, which were taller than an elephant could reach, even if she stretched her trunk up as high as it could go. However, if she stood at the far end of her enclosure and looked across, she could just make out some of the nearest cages and animals.

But despite not getting to see much of the zoo, Ndlovu knew of many things which had happened at the zoo over the years. Often she knew of these things because of the complex and special communication network the animals had developed, just as prisoners in a jail might do, so as to communicate from one area of the jail to another, when locked in their cells.

The animal communication network usually involved all the animals, and relied on them passing information along from cage to cage.

This sometimes meant that information was slightly or even significantly different to the original message, by the time it had been repeated many times, having been passed from cage to enclosure, across pathways, through bars, between walls, through sleeping boxes and around corners.

One particular day on a weekend, when the zoo had been very busy with human visitors, a little boy had run ahead of his mum and dad and baby sister in her buggy. His family were standing and staring intently at the mongoose enclosure, which was very popular with the human visitors. They were pointing and laughing at Shiro and the other mongooses, who tended to stand up on their hind legs to look curiously back at the human visitors. This had the amusing effect of making them seem like miniature humans, at least to the humans, who then did a lot of laughing and pointing and mimicking around this enclosure.

Every now and then a shout, loud laugh or sudden movement from one of the human visitors would frighten the mongooses, and they'd all dash into their rocky holes and sandy burrows, only to peep out again moments later, because their fear couldn't fully dampen their curiosity.

The little boy, unable to see properly over the mongoose enclosure walls and overjoyed to have space to run about, had excitedly rushed over to the elephant enclosure, but had been just that little too short to see over the wall and down inside, where Ndlovu the elephant was eating in a slow, deliberate way.

There were lots of humans of all shapes and sizes visiting the zoo that day, so you might have thought that someone would have noticed the little boy. Or at least, that's what Shiro said afterwards. She tut-tutted and shook her head in disbelief that the humans didn't watch their young as closely as she watched hers.

The little boy had jumped up and down, eager to see what was on the other side of the walls. Ndlovu was grazing on some fresh leaves which were still attached to some sawn off branches the human workers had thrown into her cage only just that morning, so didn't immediately notice the little human visitor. After all, only his head would have shown over the wall every time he jumped up high enough.

Eventually though, his animated movement caught Ndlovu's eye, and she stared up at the place where his head appeared every second or so, a little surprised by the alternating appearance and disappearance of a young human visitor's head. But the smell and taste of the fresh leaves was much more interesting to her.

Weekends were noisy and disruptive for the animals - human visitors came in their droves and shrieked and laughed and cried and moved without warning, almost constantly, throughout the daylight hours of every Saturday and Sunday.

But nevertheless the animals secretly looked forward to weekends, and this is why:

The human workers, who always seemed to be a little scarce during the week, suddenly became much more energetic on Saturday mornings, cleaning the animal cages and filling up the water containers with fresh, life-giving water.

But the best thing was they gave the animals extra food and some special treats the animals didn't get during the week.

So in addition to their usual food, Ndlovu got her leaves and tree branches, and sometimes even some root vegetables; the mongooses got some dried worms; the monkeys got some extra fruit including bananas; and Kolobe the warthog got some vegetables too.

Kolobe insisted that the human workers only did this to "impress" the human visitors, who were most frequent on weekends. But Shiro, once she had heard what Kolobe had said, and tried to make sense of the message which seemed to be something about the human workers and "unkindness", said Kolobe was "just being cynical".

Of course, Shiro and Kolobe couldn't simply have a conversation like you and I might – their words had to be transported via the animal communication network from cage to cage. So by the time Kolobe received Shiro's reply to what he'd said, the message was that she'd said he was "rusty and whimsical".

Kolobe was a little confused by Shiro's alleged analysis of his character. He took some time to think about it before deciding how he would reply via the animal communication network.

Certainly, his cage bars were rusty in places – he

knew this because when he was needing something to do, which was quite often, he tended to chew his cage bars. Or tried to. And rusty bars didn't taste nice. It was very difficult to get his open mouth and teeth around the bars, what with the bars and wire being so close together, and his facial tusks getting in the way – so Kolobe had finally settled on licking and sucking the bars instead.

And therein lay the problem – over the seasons, rainwater and warthog spit had caused the old bars to start rusting in some places. In fact rusty bars were quite common in this little zoo in many cages. And due to their abundance across the zoo, it seemed they weren't something deemed to need much attention from the human workers.

As for being whimsical, Kolobe wasn't too sure what that meant, but it sounded like one of those floaty words which couldn't possibly apply to him. He was an animal with firm views and a love of routine, as was evidenced by his simple life in the zoo. His days during the week were all similar – and, as he would tell anyone who would listen, he liked it that way.

So he spent at least two hours every day licking his cage bars – in his mind, this activity was an important part of his day which needed to be adhered to with rigorous determination, just like his morning and afternoon naps, which took up most of the day.

~~~~~~~~~~~~~~~~~~~~~~~~~~~~

KATHRYN ROSE NEWEY

3 – Being Natural

Some of the animal enclosures, at some point in the zoo's history, had had so-called 'natural' elements added, in an attempt to make them appear more animal-friendly.

So the monkey enclosure had some grey, dead tree stumps and branches placed in such a way as to suggest real trees, and a few grey rocks strewn about.

THE ZOO ANIMALS' FARAWAY DREAM

The monkeys, with their sandy and grey coloured fur, tended to sit on these slightly raised objects in their cage, so they could see more of what was going on outside. It was common for them to sit there, almost the same colour as the rocks, and stare at nothing in particular, lost in thought.

The zebra enclosure which was next door, and bordered on the edge of the zoo so had a high wall at the back, even had this wall covered with a large poster for the full length of the wall, which showed the scene of an African savannah, complete with golden, waving grass and dotted with the occasional acacia tree.

If you looked very quickly, it appeared almost as if the zebras really lived free in that African landscape, and not in the enclosed cage in front of the poster. Except for the rips to the corners of the poster, the faded colours in the picture and the fence, which ruined the scene slightly, of course.

The penguins had a shallow pond in front of the zebra enclosure, which had been built in a roughly convoluting shape to make it appear to be like a small, natural lake. Which might have been convincing, except it was made of grey concrete and was only just deep enough in the middle for the larger penguins to wade and wallow in, or for some of the younger and smaller penguins to actually swim like penguins should.

In fact the little boy and his family had passed the penguin's pond on their way to the mongoose enclosure. They had briefly stopped next to the penguin cage, which had a waist-high fence around the outside, and included some lumpy and jagged looking concrete shapes built up all around the pond.

These were meant to imply a rocky, perhaps snowy landscape, but unfortunately they simply looked like what they were: dirty, irregular blobs of concrete, smeared here and there with some penguin feathers, food and poo.

At this point in their visit, the boy's mum and dad had tried to encourage him to have some interest in the penguins, but no one ever really stopped at the penguin enclosure for very long. The penguins, not having enough space to roam in, simply stood or lay about in their misshapen surroundings, perhaps occasionally preening their ragged feathers, but more often just napping.

The little boy had quickly got bored and dashed off to the mongoose enclosure, which had more people peering into it; his parents had stayed and pointed at the penguins, waving and moving about, trying to teach his baby sister how to say "birdie", "penguin" and "Happy Feet".

His parents and sister had then joined him at the mongoose enclosure, and whilst the boy couldn't really see much because of the throngs of people, his parents had again become fully immersed in the task of educating their baby daughter about the resident animals – in this case the "meerkats", as they called them. They didn't seem to be aware of how comical they looked to outsiders when they mimicked mongoose movements and behaviour to the delight of their baby.

It was because of this that they hadn't noticed their son running off again. He had run right across the little zoo, staring sideways and longingly at the ice-cream stand as he ran past. He was aiming for the large, curving wall at the other side of the zoo, which, because he was a little person, seemed to loom up and appeared enormously high to him, and he was curious as to what could possibly be behind such a wall.

~~~~~~~~~~~~~~~~~~~~~~~~~~~~~

Most of the animals didn't notice, or tried not to notice the human visitors. They did their best to curl up and take naps when there were lots of humans around. But the zoo was a noisy place on these days, and the humans moved quickly, shouted and laughed - seemingly without any thought for the animals.

The young humans were the most boisterous; they ran, chasing each other playfully, shrieking and laughing, screaming and shouting – without a care in the world, and certainly without any consideration for the animals. Although the animals were used to this, they tried to ignore the frightening sounds and sudden actions of the humans by tucking their heads under their bodies or wings and trying to sleep.

This probably had the opposite effect of what the animals hoped for. With many animals being motionless or appearing to be fast asleep, the human visitors were rapidly disinterested. And thus the humans made their own entertainment.

The adult humans talked loudly near to the animals (acting as if the animals weren't really there, when they were just a few feet away), swapping tales of the weather, their journey to the zoo, how expensive the tickets were, and how quickly their children had grown up. All the while ignoring the loud and very physical antics of their offspring.

The young humans made new friends with other

youngsters, played hide and seek around the animal cages, and ran, hopped, skipped and jumped all around the zoo, gleeful at all the extra space they had at their disposal, and not particularly interested in the motionless animals behind bars all around them.

Of course all the human discussions and games were regularly punctuated with the ingestion of food and drink, accompanied by the crinkling of plastic wrappers, the popping of plastic container lids, and the rustling of paper packaging, making it even more difficult for the animals to sleep.

Some animals were better at ignoring the humans than others. The monkeys had long practised sitting still and often appeared half asleep, but kept watchful eyes, as now and then the human visitors would clandestinely offer titbits and snacks through the bars - despite the rusty signs tacked to cages and walls here and there, which instructed the human visitors in no uncertain terms:

"DO NOT FEED THE ANIMALS".

When offered food gifts in this way, the monkeys would initially look around pensively, as if expecting to get into trouble; then if all was deemed to be clear they would suddenly swing, run and jump towards the piece of food, snatch it and quickly make their way back to their perch, eating on the go. Within a few seconds they were seated and appeared half asleep again, as if they'd never moved.

These performances seemed to amuse the human visitors, who would then usually want to see if the monkeys would repeat their actions. So the humans would look around furtively, perhaps checking that no human workers were near, and then offer more titbits through the bars of the monkey cage.

Which of course had the desired effect. The monkeys would do as expected, suddenly coming to life, resulting in more laughter on the part of the humans.

At least once a week, some human visitors would jokingly comment to each other how it seemed the monkeys knew exactly what they were doing - and how it looked like the monkeys were the ones training the humans! The humans would then laugh uproariously and move away, shaking their heads, sure in their superiority over all species.

~~~~~~~~~~~~~~~~~~~~~~~~~~~~

4 – Deliriously Happy

By and large, most animals didn't interact much with the human visitors though. They generally slept, or feigned sleeping or napping, as much as possible. Some had even mastered the art of sleeping through all the squeals and babbles and howls that the humans, especially the young humans, made when they visited the zoo.

At times this was even more difficult, especially if the humans were also eating food that smelt really appetising to the animals; the aromas would dance around the animals' nostrils and the temptations were sometimes too much to bear.

But the animals knew by now that no matter how good the human food was, in most cases they were not going to get a share of it.

The zebras, being a little skittish, found it impossible to remain completely unresponsive to the humans. They frequently flicked their ears and tails, and snorted and lifted and lowered their heads, whenever there was intrusive human activity.

When it was quiet for a moment or two, they'd dip down to quickly nibble on some grass or hay; but their peace didn't last as one of the humans might suddenly talk or knock something over or push up against someone or call out for their lost child.

There wasn't much space for the three zebras to run in. They'd trot a short way, only to have to turn around and trot the other way. As such they were at times quite sedentary, because they often felt that there was no point in trotting. It didn't get them anywhere.

But every now and then one of them would get a sudden burst of energy, as if they couldn't help it, kick their hind legs up and try to gallop across their small enclosure.

But of course it was all to no avail, because within seconds they were at the fence and had to turn around. All this activity would get the other two zebras excited too, so for a short and manic moment they'd also have a fierce rush, which culminated within a few moments in all three of them crashing into each other, or the fence, or both.

~~~~~~~~~~~~~~~~~~~~~~~~~~~~~

Kolobe the warthog was trying to use the time during his half-naps, while ignoring the human visitors, to continue considering what Shiro the mongoose had said. He wasn't sure if she was being rude or complimentary in describing him in that way, but he thought some sort of response had to be given.

Shiro wasn't the type of animal to take nonsense from anyone – she was the zoo's self-imposed matriarch, and most of the animals, males and females alike, would listen to her. But equally,

Kolobe felt that if she was wrong, and indeed it seemed this time she might be, then it had to be said.

So Kolobe thought about his reply carefully. She had called him "rusty and whimsical", and he wasn't sure what she'd based that on. In fact he didn't even know if she'd understood that he was commenting about the human workers. But if her reply wasn't clear to him – and he regarded himself as a smart animal – then it couldn't be true. She was mistaken. And that was that.

Once the zoo was quiet again, with all the human visitors and workers having gone home for the day, he called to Ndlovu the elephant, whose enclosed pit was next to his.

Ndlovu didn't immediately reply, but Kolobe could hear her moving in the darkness. Kolobe could hear a faint swishing noise, which sounded like it is was coming from Ndlovu's cage. He stopped to listen, cocking his head, tusks and warts and all. There was definitely a sound of movement, like someone swaying backwards and forwards, and from Ndlovu's direction.

He called out to her again. The sounds stopped. Then Ndlovu started speaking, and even Kolobe, who wasn't one to bother too much with emotions, thought she sounded a little hesitant.

"Sorry, Kolobe, I was a little distracted… I think".

"What's happening?" said Kolobe, momentarily worried that she had not sounded like that before.

"Oh…nothing…really" said Ndlovu, but she was still unsure of herself.

However Kolobe, not being particularly skilled in the

art of perceiving other's feelings, turned to his own problem.

"Well," he said, "could you tell Shiro from me that I am most definitely *not* rusty and whimsical. In fact, I take offence. Shiro ought to know better. I am, after all, a very simple animal, and I like things to be uncomplicated. That's what life is all about – how to be uncomplicated. That's how you know it's working – if things stay the same, day after day…"

He was getting a little carried away, and Ndlovu had to interrupt him.

"Kolobe! I will tell her", she simply said, and then walked, a little slower than she usually did, to the wall of her enclosure which was closest to the parrots' cage.

The message was then transmitted along the animal

communication network, via all the cages between Kolobe and the mongooses, from Ndlovu (who was feeling a little weary, so might have edited the message to what she thought were just the significant bits), to the parrots (who, being very chatty, liked to embellish messages with their own interpretations and additions), to Noko the porcupine (who was quite shy and didn't really like to give messages, so he may have inadvertently cut out most of what the parrots said), and finally to the mongoose enclosure.

Shiro got the message the next morning: Kolobe's reply to her was that she was "dense and not constipated".

~~~~~~~~~~~~~~~~~~~~~~~~~~~~~

5 – A Visitor

One morning, Noko the porcupine, whose cage was next door to the mongooses, was woken up to tinkering, snuffling and knocking sounds. At first he opened his eyes slowly, thinking it must be the human workers – perhaps it was the weekend again and they were giving him extra food?

He sniffed hopefully, but smelt something strange – definitely not any food he was interested in. Then there was a little clink and he leapt up in fright.

A small creature with dark brown, smooth fur was sniffing around his cage and drinking his water! Or the little bit of dirty water left in his bowl which might not be replenished for another day or two. He bristled in annoyance.

Being a porcupine, when he felt under attack, his quills would stand more upright. They were meant to deter any other creature from coming too close – and caused painful wounds if anyone did get too close, as the quills came loose and would easily embed in another animal's nose, face or skin, and were then very difficult to remove. Noko felt his quills rising slightly.

"What are you doing here?" he asked. "Why are you not in your own cage?"

Radati the rat laughed. And laughed some more. He laughed almost as if he couldn't stop laughing.

At first Noko didn't understand that the creature was laughing. After all, laughing wasn't something the animals in this zoo did too often.

But then Noko realized the sounds coming from the creature were indeed that strange and infrequently heard thing: laughter.

"Why are you laughing?" he demanded stiffly. His quills quivered and rose a little more. "This isn't a funny moment!"

This statement only caused Radati to laugh some more, which made Noko shrink with discomfort at the stranger's audacity. Radati continued to sniff and walk about Noko's cage, in careless disregard for the owner, as if he had lived there all his life.

"I am Radati the rat" he announced. "I don't live in a cage!

"I am free: free to walk into your cage and take your food and water, and free to leave and go elsewhere if I want to!"

Noko was shocked and horrified, then confused. He didn't know what to say. Not only was this animal very rude and blunt, but Noko had never met an animal who didn't have a cage.

The human workers and visitors were different, so they didn't count as animals, he felt. He cocked his head to one side.

Humans usually didn't seem to feel and think like the animals did – they seemed to be preoccupied or distant, and it appeared to him they didn't properly 'see' the animals in the cages, even when they were looking directly at them.

And then there were birds and insects who also didn't generally live in cages. He was partial to occasionally snacking on insects. Pity there were so few tasty ones around his cage.

All the animals knew that there were birds both in the zoo, including the parrots and penguins, and outside, like sparrows and crows and pigeons, who were free to fly about. The noisy parrots in the small rectangular cage next door to Noko's cage seemed to talk a lot, almost like humans. But then they had wings and beaks and two feet, like the penguins at the other end of the zoo, so he knew they were birds.

THE ZOO ANIMALS' FARAWAY DREAM

It was just one of those things – some birds were in cages, like the zoo animals were, and other birds were not. So in the animals' minds, those free birds weren't regarded as proper animals. After all, real animals lived in cages, didn't they?

Noko felt as if he was getting very muddled, thinking about animals, birds and cages. Life would be simpler if all animals and birds were in cages, he felt.

But now here was this extraordinary rat animal, who had somehow appeared in Noko's cage, and who claimed he didn't have his own cage! It was all terribly perturbing.

Or at least the rat seemed to be more of an animal (with fur, a twitching nose, four legs and a tail), than a human. And he certainly wasn't a bird or an insect. Besides, Noko could understand him when he spoke, so the rat must be an animal, surely?

Noko stared at Radati, but turned away when he realized he was at a loss as to what to say. And even though Noko was both alarmed and amazed by this intruder, he didn't think it right to stare directly at him for too long.

Radati seemed to soften slightly; perhaps he actually felt sorry for Noko.

"You've never seen an animal who doesn't live in a cage?" he asked.

"No," said Noko, "I haven't."

"Well, if you let me finish my meal, I promise I will explain it all to you", Radati said, chewing on a peach pip.

Noko didn't think the creature should refer to the food in his cage as '*my* meal', as if the creature had been given that food by the human workers, and as if the rat was an animal in a cage like all the other animals.

But Noko couldn't say anything; he felt too insecure and flustered. So instead he waited patiently, trying not to notice how the creature was eating up most of his food, and curious as to what this rat creature would say.

Once Radati had eaten up all the tasty last few bits of fruit in Noko's cage, and sipped some water, he found a comfy spot in the corner and curled up, as if he was about to go to sleep.

"Er... Rat... you were going to tell me about... about not living in a cage?" Noko asked tentatively.

But Radati was asleep, snoring softly, and Noko, not being proficient enough in communication skills for these sorts of situations, left him to sleep.

Noko lay down tentatively at the other end of his cage, keeping one eye on the creature in case he should wake up.

It seemed a little colder in his cage and he looked up through his cage bars. He could see the ever-present clouds, who, in their eagerness to prove their superiority over the sun, scrabbled around the sky in strange patterns, then closed in, slicing into and suffocating each other. The poor sun, always one against many, didn't stand a chance.

The clouds, insistent on making everything grey and miserable, started pouring rain down on the little zoo, and Noko shivered.

~~~~~~~~~~~~~~~~~~~~~~~~~~~~~

6 – *Sweet Redemption*

The little boy had somehow managed to hoist himself up onto the wall of Ndlovu the elephant's enclosure. There were lots of humans walking past, some stopping and pointing at the elephant in the pit below, but initially no one spotted the boy.

Ndlovu continued eating. She was used to the interruptions by extra humans on the weekends, and tried her best to focus on enjoying her additional, more tasty food, whilst ignoring the humans who endlessly talked and walked and laughed and pointed and shouted and jumped and cried and screamed around her enclosure all day long for the two busiest days.

Before the next person could say 'elephant', the little boy had pulled himself up onto the wall and began walking slowly along it, with his arms stretched out for balance.

"Look at me, mum and dad!" he shouted in glee.

Unfortunately for him, not everyone was as happy as he was. A woman gasped then screamed, someone shouted "look out", and a mother let her own child's hand go in order to reach out frantically to the boy.

The boy's mum and dad, still cooing and gargling at

their baby daughter outside the mongoose enclosure, heard the commotion and eventually realised it involved one of their own offspring. They rushed over to the elephant enclosure in a panic, with their daughter bouncing in the buggy as they pushed it speedily towards the disturbance.

Ndlovu paused with eating her tasty leaves, and looked up at the unfolding scene, blinking because she sensed that something out of the ordinary was about to unfold.

The little boy was too caught up in what he was doing to see or hear the outcry all around him. So he kept sliding his feet along the wall, with his arms outspread like wings. He had taken a few steps and was feeling more confident, so was beginning to speed up.

He had so far managed to evade the outstretched arms of some adult humans who thought he shouldn't be walking along a wall with an elephant below him, partly because their grasps were hesitant and ineffective - because after all, he wasn't their child, and they didn't know if they should interfere or not.

His mother and father, with his little sister in her buggy, were now struggling to break through the murmuring and chattering crowd which had gathered around the elephant enclosure.

Then, as if in slow motion, one of the little boy's feet missed their step, and he teetered, horribly close to edge of the open elephant enclosure. A few women screamed in unison.

"Whoa" said the little boy, no longer as confident as

before; a new uncertainty and fear had crept into his voice.

The woman who had let her own child go grabbed at one of his hands, but missed. Then another man rushed forward, tripping over the little girl who had been temporarily abandoned by her mother, and launched face-first into the wall.

The little girl whose mother had left her wailed in fright and indignation; not only had her mum let her go but now some horrid, large man had kicked at her and had fallen on top of her too.

Everyone in the immediate vicinity stopped what they were doing and rushed over, not really looking where they were going, all wanting to be the one who saved the boy. Two more people crashed into each other and tripped over the man and little girl already rolling and crying on the ground.

As the little boy on the wall staggered about momentarily and it appeared as if he would fall towards the pit below, his mother and father simultaneously screamed his name in disbelief. They had managed to barrage their way into the middle of the group, but now their daughter's buggy was between them and the wall.

Finally a tall man with dreadlocks flailing pushed forward, over the rabble of wriggling, whining bodies, and firmly pulled the little boy off the wall to safety. The little boy landed with a loud bump on the ground at his parents' feet; they grabbed him and immediately started admonishing him in front of everyone.

His arm was sore where he had been clutched by his

saviour, and he had a grazed and bleeding knee. He rubbed his arm and started crying in shock and embarrassment.

"Dylan, I told you to stay with me!" wailed his mum, now crying too.

"That's it, Dylan," shouted his dad, wagging his finger at him, "NO MORE ZOOS FOR YOU!"

This had the effect of increasing the distress of both Dylan and his mum, who were now sobbing even more loudly. His little sister, sensing tension, joined in and began crying too, whilst straining against the straps which held her in her buggy. But if anyone had bothered to listen to her, they would have heard her begging "wanna go wall too".

The lady had found her little lost girl and was hugging her, stroking her hair to reassure her.

"Mummy's here, don't worry pumpkin", she said, and then, as if an after-thought, asked the boy if he was alright.

Dylan nodded slightly, alternating between crying and looking up with wide eyes at all the people grouped around him in a big circle.

The dreadlocks man, still breathing hard from his super-hero moment, looked from mum to dad to little boy, then leaned in at the little boy and whispered conspiratorially "That was some trip, wasn't it?"

The little boy nodded, then smiled a little and stopped crying. His mum and dad, now self-conscious because everyone was watching them with slightly disapproving faces, tried to soften what they were saying.

THE ZOO ANIMALS' FARAWAY DREAM

"Er, thanks" said Dylan's dad, clumsily shaking the dreadlock man's hand.

"It was nothing", replied the dreadlocks man. "You'd have done the same for me."

Dylan's dad looked away for a moment, uncomfortable that all eyes were on him, perhaps expecting him to offer some platitudes in return.

"Come on, Dylan" said his mum, "let's get you some ice-cream and sweeties".

As they led him towards the refreshments hut, safely ensconced between them and with each parent holding firmly onto one of his hands, he looked over his shoulder and asked "Why did that man have snakes in his hair?"

~~~~~~~~~~~~~~~~~~~~~~~~~~~~~

7 – *The Faraway Dream*

Shiro the mongoose, ever vigilant about the habits of the zoo animals and how these contributed to everyone's happiness, felt it her duty to have a serious conversation with the zebras. Shiro, who had observed them doing a lot of trotting and bumping into each other and their cage, was concerned that the zebras were not behaving as they should, or as she felt all zoo animals should.

She felt very strongly that all the animals in the zoo should be positive and happy, or at least be outwardly cheerful. It was imperative, she felt, that no animal, through thoughtless and selfish behaviour, should make other animals unhappy.

Luckily for her, the mongoose enclosure was next door to the zebras' fenced in area, so Shiro could shout across from the top of the pile of rocks in her enclosure, and the zebras, if pressed against the fence on the side of their cage closest to the mongooses, could just about hear her.

They daren't not come to the fence if called, because Shiro, albeit small, was a formidable figure and when she spoke, the others paid attention for fear of getting into trouble if they didn't.

So one evening, after the human workers had gone home for the day, Shiro climbed up to the top of the mongoose's stone hill and called shrilly across to the zebras.

"Zebras, come closer to me" she said in an insistent but squeaky voice which gave no room for resistance, "I must speak with you".

The three zebras looked up, surprised by Shiro's sudden interest in them. At that moment, the clouds bunched together and tossed some soft rain down on the little zoo. The zebras would have preferred to go into their shed and huddle together to keep dry and warm, but they knew it was better to obey her. They complied by trotting over to the side of their cage closest to her, and waited, with feelings of trepidation. 'What was it that Shiro wanted now?' they wondered.

"Honestly zebras," began Shiro, a little crossly, "I think you ought to be more careful in what you do."

The zebras looked at the ground, a little confused about what she was referring to, but not daring to question her at this stage.

"I'm perturbed that you're upsetting some of the other animals with your silly running about in your cage" continued Shiro.

The zebras, who were used to Shiro's frequent overbearing ways due to the unfortunate positioning of their cage right next door to the mongoose enclosure, could only feel a little downcast and embarrassed by Shiro's criticism.

"We'll try harder", whispered Dube, the oldest of the

three, pawing the ground with his hoof. He shook his mane and some water droplets flew in all directions.

"It's just that…" started Goreb, but then trailed off because Shiro was looking intently at her. Goreb looked at Dube for support, but he was looking away.

Mbizi, the youngest, pushed her way to the fence and boldly declared "But it's what we do!"

Being young, Mbizi had perhaps not yet learnt to take extra care with what she said in front of Shiro.

She shook her head, almost defiantly it seemed, and her black and white mane undulated up and down her neck. It caused some raindrops to fan out, with some flying straight into Goreb's face; who shook her mane and ears in agitation and almost lost her balance.

"Now Mbizi", chastised Shiro in a disapproving and loud voice (or as loud as a high-pitched voice from a small animal could be), "you know we *must* all be happy here. You need to consider that."

She paused, glaring intently with shiny black eyes at Mbizi, who stared back.

"I don't want the penguins, monkeys or capybaras getting flustered from your childish antics again!"

Of course Shiro considered the matter closed. She climbed down the rocky pile swiftly, then tried to keep her dignity when she started sliding (due to the soft rain running down), all the while mumbling to herself. Once the zebras were sure she couldn't see them anymore, they clustered in their shed at the far end of the zebra cage, which was furthest away from the mongoose enclosure, and whispered together.

There was something they had discussed amongst themselves a few times before. It was a strange thing; it was a thing that they wanted to hide from but were drawn to. And somehow they knew that the running about in their cage had something to do with this thing.

The first time they had ever talked about it was when Goreb had woken up with a fright during the night and had sobbed uncontrollably.

When she had insisted she had been running free in a grassy plain with sunshine on her back, Dube and Mbizi had tried to placate her. They had looked at each other, over her back, with worried glances, especially as they were all quite obviously in a cage in a zoo, and it was night time.

THE ZOO ANIMALS' FARAWAY DREAM

But the dream of running free would not be put away easily. And then it started happening to Dube and Mbizi too.

Some might say perhaps it was the stimulus of the African savannah poster across the wall of the zebra enclosure which had put fanciful ideas in their heads. Others might believe it was just something beating in the zebras' veins or hearts, as every few weeks one or more of the zebras had vivid imaginings of galloping and frolicking on a dusty grassland dotted with trees and shrubs.

Sometimes they even dreamt of other animals there too – large and strange horned beasts, nimble reddish brown and white coloured creatures, and lots of other zebras.

The most amazing thing, as the zebras realised from

talking amongst themselves in hushed tones, was that there were never any fences in their dreams.

And almost without thinking about it, the zebras somehow knew inherently that it was probably at least partly because of these dreams that they would get sudden bursts of energy, seemingly for no particular reason, which lead to them prancing in a "childish" way, as Shiro put it, and not being able to avoid colliding into each other and their fence because of their uninhibited exuberance.

~~~~~~~~~~~~~~~~~~~~~~~~~~~

8 – *The Faraway Nightmare*

Unbeknown to the zebras, the dream of being free wasn't that uncommon amongst the other zoo animals.

The monkeys, in their quieter moments - which as you know was quite often because there wasn't much to do in their cage - liked to immerse themselves in daydreaming about lush jungles with wonderful tasting berries, seeds, flowers and fruits.

If you looked really carefully while they were perched on the rocks and branches in their cage, apparently asleep, you might very occasionally notice their toes twitching, their tails curling, or a slight quivering of their lips.

Now the monkeys did not have the benefit of a large poster in their cage depicting their natural habitat, as the zebras did. So what was it that caused this longing?

Ndlovu the elephant, too, couldn't shake off a persistent reverie where she was moving serenely through a treed landscape with other elephants, uprooting some branches and roots to eat and slurping up water with her trunk from a giant pool in the sunshine, with other animals roaming freely around them.

Even Kolobe the warthog had found himself every now and then sinking into quiet meditation, where he was happily wandering in a savannah and it seemed so real he had to shake his head and body hard to check it wasn't.

Of course Kolobe, being an animal who was absolutely sure about what life was all about, simply put it down to his creeping old age or blamed the other animals, who must have secretly encouraged him to be out of touch with reality, as he felt they so often were.

With the result that Kolobe didn't feel himself slipping into the dream so much anymore. But these things cannot simply be eradicated from one's mind, no matter how determined the animal is. So when Kolobe was asleep, just sometimes his brain would still tease him with beautiful, dusty landscapes, other warthogs, mud to wallow in, and lots of fat, tasty roots and insects.

~~~~~~~~~~~~~~~~~~~~~~~~~~~~

These dreams were bewildering to the animals who experienced them, so they tended not to mention them too much along the animal communication network. In any case, their words might simply be amended, twisted or mangled into something else, as was so often the case with the animal communication network.

As indeed had happened that fateful day when the little boy had almost fallen into Ndlovu's enclosure.

Kolobe, whose cage was closest to the action, had

reported the story in detail to the other animals. It was an unusual event so the story had travelled around the zoo more than once, from cage to cage, and even the tortoise and lizards, whose small enclosures were towards the exit of the zoo, had heard it a few times.

The story was an opportunity for the animals to talk about something other than their cages, food or water for once, hence its popularity.

Kolobe, keen to report the truth, had stated how a little human had climbed up onto Ndlovu's wall and was trying to fly, how the older human visitors had all screamed at him and had rushed to the wall to do the same but had fallen over each other in a stampede, how eventually the little human had started flying but had slipped and had almost fallen into Ndlovu's pit, how an older human with straw for hair had pulled the little human away before he fell, and how this had caused consternation on the part of all the humans who seemed to think the little human should have been allowed to fly.

Kulak the caracal, whose cage was one of the few in the middle of the zoo, and situated between the penguin pond, the mongoose enclosure and Kolobe's cylindrical cage, had also been witness to the event. But Kulak had been a fairly young caracal at the time, so although Kolobe's account of the young human's actions wasn't quite what she felt had really happened, she hadn't said anything because Kolobe was, after all, regarded as a matter-of-fact animal, or so he claimed himself many times - so surely he wouldn't embellish anything?

It was the reporting of the young human flying that she had issue with. She had seen him climbing up onto Ndlovu's wall and walking along it with her own eyes. As for flying - well that's what birds did, not humans.

Being a caracal, she knew about climbing. Luckily there was an elevated old tree branch stretched right across her cage, so she was able to jump up onto it and climb to the topmost part most nights and look out into the darkness, while the other animals were sleeping.

The tree branch, one of those supposed 'natural elements' added by the human workers, also facilitated one of her favourite, but necessarily secret, occupations – staring at the mongooses (which she might catch a glimpse of every now and then, over their enclosure wall) and licking her lips. This was not something she could readily admit to anyone, because she didn't fully understand the nature of her obsession with the mongooses and her compulsive, but pleasant, imaginings of what the flesh under their fur might taste like.

Kulak was the only carnivore in the little zoo, and like most things in this zoo, the human workers were not inclined to spend too much time or waste money on anything regarded as too costly.

Thus once a week, which seemed to coincide with the days most human visitors appeared, Kulak was given chopped up baby chickens as the meat part of her food, rather than anything more extravagant. This meat was mixed in with what she usually ate on other days - lots of small, round, grainy pellets, which had a slight meaty smell that evaporated upon chewing them.

But somehow even the meat she was given wasn't

completely satisfying, and her meat 'treat' didn't seem to reduce her drooling whilst gazing at the mongoose enclosure.

~~~~~~~~~~~~~~~~~~~~~~~~~~~~~

The story of the young human on Ndlovu's wall had been around the animal communication network a few times, and when the final version arrived back at Kulak's cage again, Kulak simply laughed out loud.

Of course, laughter was not something that happened very often in the little zoo. So when she laughed, most of the other animals simply assumed it was her calling out to the evening sky.

The story which had amused her so much, eventually retold to her by the capybaras, went something like this:

"The little human appeared on Ndlovu's wall, crying

goodbye. The adult human visitors, all suffering from cramped knees, had brushed the small human.

"The little human had wanted to die, because he'd heard a ghost calling him in Ndlovu's pit.

"The adults, struggling with dehydration, had pawed the air. They had felt fooled, and wanted to drink. They all said out aloud that the young human should cry."

~~~~~~~~~~~~~~~~~~~~~~~~~~~~

9 – A Terrible Thing

Two of the monkeys awoke with a start. An unusual sound, not typical of night time, had stirred them.

They listened carefully and made soft, whining sounds to each other, trying to peer out into the darkness to identify what had woken them.

Noises at night weren't that unusual. Some of the

animals in the zoo were awake for some or all of the night, so they could be heard wandering and snuffling about their cages or calling out, and quite often there were strange, high-pitched or rumbling sounds of barking, screeching and howling coming from outside the zoo.

But these sounds were different.

Then there was a louder sound, and some jiggling and banging sounds. Now all of the monkeys were awake, as these noises were closest to their cage. One or two of the younger monkeys moved to the back of their cage and held onto each other for reassurance, trembling and mumbling.

Human voices! That's what they could hear. But not the usual loud, confident voices of human workers or visitors. These voices were quieter, with a whistling quality to them, as if the humans making them were trying to not be heard.

The monkeys sniffed the air. In the cold of the night, they could smell the humans – their sweat, the recent meals on their breaths, and a mix of something else, as if the humans were both apprehensive and excited.

Then there was a clang, which woke up most of the animals in other cages near to the monkeys, and the sound of a human cheering, with others giggling.

The monkeys could just make out some human shapes moving quickly past their cage into the middle part of the zoo. They strained to see what was happening, but at the same time sensed this was not a good thing. They shrivelled in the back of their cage, their fear and curiosity battling each other.

The human silhouettes seemed to be pause for a minute, talking, chuckling and sniggering. There was some sort of discussion, with one or two louder voices rising now and then, while others shushed them and laughed.

Then they made their way over to the penguin pond.

Most of the zoo animals were now peering out into the darkness to see what was going on. Those animals that were nocturnal could of course see much better in the dark than those who weren't, but even so, the human shapes and noises seemed to move about and not everyone could discern what they were doing.

There were various knocking and rattling sounds, and next thing, the penguins were quacking and squawking and moaning, with lots of wing flapping.

They were clearly frightened and sounded as if they were trying to escape.

The listening animals froze; their hearts beat loudly in their chests and their tongues suddenly felt dry in their mouths.

But even louder than that were the sounds of the humans shouting, hooting and chortling - which all the animals in the zoo, now awake and very alarmed, could hear.

The monkeys started crying out and howling, which started the zebras running up and down their enclosure in consternation, crashing into each other and snorting. The capybaras barked and whined and ran in endless circles in their cage, responding to the general turmoil.

Even the animals at the other end of the zoo were

now awake and crying out, which only made it all worse – anyone not wailing was soon doing so after they heard every other animal's distressed calls.

The humans were still in the zoo, bashing about, talking and laughing. Their activities seemed impervious to the animals' anguish – in fact, the animals' obvious fear only seemed to make the humans laugh and shout more boldly.

Then one of the humans tripped over something, stumbled and fell. The others guffawed at him, pulled him to his feet, and they ran out of the zoo, clanging the gate after them.

Their laughter and shouts echoed in the night air, but were not distinguishable from the troubled animals' outpourings.

It took a while for there to be quiet again; there were

so many animals bawling and yapping and cawing and shrieking that at first they didn't realise the humans had gone.

Slowly the animal sounds died down, until just the penguins were mumbling and squawking.

The animals who usually slept at night took a long while to settle and when they did, they had fitful nightmares of humans chasing and beating them with sticks.

~~~~~~~~~~~~~~~~~~~~~~~~~~~~~

Some early rays of light started to creep into the small zoo, very cautiously, as if they knew there was trouble and they didn't want to take the blame. The clouds, never ones to lose, simply moved in and hung over everything, shadowing and darkening the scene. But despite their efforts, even the smallest amount of daylight was enough to reveal the full extent of the previous night's disaster.

The penguins' cage fencing was loose, broken and dangling in places, with some sharp edges sticking up, and at least four of the penguins were outside their cage, wandering around the zoo in bewilderment.

They looked dishevelled; most of the penguins' feathers were messy and sticking out at angles where they should be smoother on their bodies. There were also lots of feathers, other items and dirt scattered about on the ground, blowing about in the soft morning breeze.

The penguins' food containers were tipped up, with food randomly dispersed all over outside their cage. One of the escapee penguins, who had managed to out-run the humans, was trying to get his share of the spilt food but was having to vie with a few pigeons who had landed next to the unexpected offering and were greedily gobbling it up.

~~~~~~~~~~~~~~~~~~~~~~~~~~~~

10 – Being Free

Radati the rat stretched and yawned languidly, as if he had slept well, then opened his eyes. Noko, still in awe of him, was lying in the far corner of his cage, eyeing him warily.

"Ah, there you are", said Radati. "I must say, you have a comfortable cage." His eyes twinkled when he said this.

Noko the porcupine looked about his small cage - the rusting bars close together which stopped him leaving (but were wide enough for the rat creature to walk in and out), the dirty water bowl, the fruit pips and a few bits of food the rat had not yet eaten strewn about, dirt and dust everywhere and even some dry leaves collected in the corners, and the little wooden box, worn and chewed on the edges, which provided shelter for him.

Noko nodded politely, but really didn't think his cage was exceedingly comfortable or in any way an outstanding example amongst cages. After all, the mongoose enclosure next to his seemed larger because it housed a whole community of mongooses, and the parrot cage on the other side was taller than his cage, offering the parrots a better view.

"Er, yes", said Noko, trying to be agreeable, because he wanted to hear what the rat had to say about not living in a cage.

"So you want to know about cages," smiled Radati, "or rather, how come I don't live in a cage?"

He smiled a little, as if this idea was still amusing to him.

"Yes please….er…Rat…" said Noko, creeping a little closer to the creature and looking directly at him for a moment, as if he didn't quite believe the 'no cage' statement, but couldn't help being inquisitive.

By now some of the mongooses had grouped close to the wall facing Noko's cage to listen to this stranger's amazing tale, and the parrots had shuffled along the one branch across the top of their cage to hear the story.

Radati shook his ears and nibbled on some scraps of food. The others waited patiently with baited breaths.

When Radati was finally ready, he started telling Noko how he, along with his brother and sister rats, had been born in a nest, in a place underground, some way from the zoo in the outside world.

He explained how his mother rat had looked after them, shown them how to find food and water, and once the babies had all grown up, some had remained with their mother and a community of other rats, while Radati and some of his brothers had left to explore the outside world.

Then he paused, perhaps to emphasize the

significant effect of what he was saying to the caged animals. Or perhaps it was because he had spotted a beetle walking along the cage bars and lunged at it, eating it with relish, while Noko watched him, wondering if he would like to eat some of it too, but too polite to ask.

Noko was thinking carefully about what this rat creature was saying. It seemed too far-fetched to believe.

And yet, at the same time, it seemed almost familiar to him. Suddenly his thoughts were interrupted with a vivid memory of being a baby porcupine in a nest with two siblings, and a mother and father who had cared for them, lovingly bringing them up.

He started shaking and Radati stopped eating for a moment, looking at him questioningly.

THE ZOO ANIMALS' FARAWAY DREAM

Noko turned away momentarily with tears in his eyes. He was confused. It felt so real, and yet, how could that be? And how did he get from there, to here in this zoo?

He lifted his head with his eyes closed, as if he wanted to call back those images. But then he recollected where he was, and that Radati, and the other animals, were waiting.

"I'm sorry," Noko said hurriedly, "but I just had the most strangest and wonderful dream. At least, I think it was a dream…"

Then he shook his head rapidly, as if to clear that memory or dream or whatever it was from his brain. He looked around his cage, and pressed his padded feet firmly into the straw and dust on the floor, reminding himself that this was where he was, and this was all there was.

"My friend," said Radati, nodding in a knowing way, "what you are experiencing is the faraway dream."

~~~~~~~~~~~~~~~~~~~~~~~~~~~~~

Radati was talking again.

He explained how rats and many other animals, including birds, foxes, badgers, deer, hedgehogs and so on, all lived in fields and forests freely, without cages.

He also mentioned some other animals - cows, sheep, pigs and chickens - who were partly free, he explained. He said sometimes they were allowed out to eat in large fields, but human workers and their dogs came to get them at night and put them in buildings or cages to sleep in.

The zoo animals were quiet, mulling this surprising

information over.

One of the older mongooses, who was sceptical of this seemingly ridiculous report, shouted out "but who feeds the free ones?"

Radati laughed out loud. The animals looked at each other in confusion. Some of the mongooses thought Radati was being a bit rude. After all, not many animals in the zoo laughed, but wasn't laughter supposed to be for when something was actually amusing? 'Wherever he came from,' they thought, 'he obviously didn't learn manners.'

"All of us free animals feed ourselves" Radati said, in a matter-of-fact way.

"We look for food, and eat throughout the day, or some of us prefer at night. Our food grows in the fields and forests, and sometimes humans leave food out which they don't want, so we eat it."

This statement created a stir. The mongooses all chatted amongst themselves, incredulous that animals could walk around freely and find food for themselves.

One of the younger mongooses, known for being 'otherwise', insisted that if humans were leaving food out, then they were feeding the animals, just like in the zoo, so really, those animals weren't free – but no one was listening to her.

Shiro had joined the little group of mongooses pressed against the wall now. She stood her ground, while the others jostled to get a better position, closer to the wall and where they could hear the stranger's enlightening tales.

"Mongooses, he doesn't know what he's talking

about!" she declared determinedly, but this time the other mongooses didn't seem to take much notice of her. She went on and on, insisting and moaning, not used to being ignored.

She knew she had to urgently protect everyone against these insinuations that animals could be free and look after themselves, and perhaps even become happier than they were in the zoo.

She was resolute that nothing, not even this creature from the outside world and his silly talk of impossible freedom, would disturb the carefully crafted illusion. Well, it wasn't entirely an illusion, she felt. After all, she and the other mongooses were happy, she was sure of it, but she knew that some of the other animals had to be cajoled into happiness from time to time.

Despite her protests this time, the mongooses stayed bunched up together against the wall, listening attentively to everything the rat had to say. Shiro tried to pull them away, and implored them to come and lie in the sunshine (the little bit of sunshine that had momentarily and wearily reached out it's rays before the disagreeable clouds noticed) – but this time, they didn't obey.

The parrots, pushing against each other on their branch, chattered and trilled in amazement too. Then without warning, two of the older parrots suddenly found themselves talking at the same time, about a time when they had lived in a luscious green forest and found fruits and seeds to feed themselves.

They chuckled in a confused way when they realised what they were doing, because they didn't understand how or why this could be. It felt like a

THE ZOO ANIMALS' FARAWAY DREAM

memory, but seemed more dreamlike.

Then they became quiet, because the imaginary thing was good, and they wished they were there again. They looked around their dirty, barred cage with renewed sadness, and inched along their perch, straining to feel some of the reluctant sunlight on their ruffled, faded feathers.

~~~~~~~~~~~~~~~~~~~~~~~~~~~

11 –A True Leader

The animals had become quite perplexed by the whole incident where the little boy almost fell or flew into Ndlovu the elephant's pit (depending what they had heard or who they'd believed), especially by the reactions of the human workers.

Immediately afterwards, once the little boy had been

led away by his parents, some animals witnessed - and duly reported it later to the others via the animal communication network – how some human workers had rushed up to the scene, and had shouted and waved their arms about, indicating the human visitors should all leave.

It took a long time for all the human visitors to gather up their children, belongings and food items, and for them to make their way, grumbling and fumbling and talking in hushed tones, or loud and angry voices, about what had happened with the little boy and everyone's subsequent hasty and premature exit.

On their way out, the human visitors complained about how the zoo workers should have arrived on the scene sooner and done something, how the zoo should have had better safety procedures, how every other zoo they had visited was better than this one in countless ways, how the elephant would almost certainly have killed the little boy had he fallen in, how the other cages weren't safe for humans either, how this zoo housed many dangerous and vicious animals with ineffective and unsafe barriers - and generally how terrible, inconvenient, unfair and preposterous the whole situation was for them that day.

When all the visitors had been ushered out of the zoo, the human workers stood about discussing what had just happened.

To the animals who could see them, it appeared like many other times when the human workers gathered together: there was lots of talking, laughing, some shouting and some exuberance, and not a lot of attending to the animals, such as feeding them or cleaning their cages.

The animals often wished the human workers would take a little less time talking and laughing, and a little more time ministering to their needs.

The rest of that day had then been quiet – an unusual and pleasant surprise for the animals, who had expected, as per the normal routine, that the human visitors and all the noise, chaos, food smells and disruption they brought, would have stayed for a few more hours, and would have been repeated the next day.

But the zoo remained free of human visitors for a few days in a row.

Then suddenly one morning, there was a burst of activity.

The human workers all came in, cleaned out the

animal cages - it seemed more thoroughly than most other times, or so Kolobe asserted - and gave the animals fresh food and water.

Kulak had been cynical too – not only had the human workers woken her up when she was sleeping, as was normal for her to do during the day, because they took longer to clean her cage than usual, but the food they dished up seemed to have been more carefully prepared, and there was more of it than they might give on other days.

While most of the animals were relishing this favourable situation (and expecting that the human visitors might be arriving soon), Shiro was doing her best to insist to the mongooses and anyone else nearby that "this was nothing exceptional, it was just how the human workers always did things."

THE ZOO ANIMALS' FARAWAY DREAM

Towards the middle of the morning, along with some rain, some new human workers appeared. They had carried in lots of boxes, equipment, poles and rolls of mesh wire, and made their way to Ndlovu's enclosure.

Ndlovu was enjoying some vegetables and leafy branches, in addition to her usual hay, for her breakfast. It was such a pleasant experience that she stood outside, happily eating, not even noticing the light rain which plopped and plunked onto her large back.

She looked up in surprise as the human workers appeared at the high wall above her enclosure, talking, pointing, nodding or shaking their heads and generally making lots of hand movements.

One of them held some sort of large piece of paper

in his hands, and occasionally they would all pore over it. Every now and then they would shake it impatiently to remove the rain drops which had fallen onto it and threatened to ruin their day.

The animals noticed that the paper bearing human seemed important, as the other humans stopped talking when he spoke, and they bustled about him, doing his bidding whenever he asked. Kolobe even claimed that when the important human had turned in his direction, he was sure he had seen tusks; after all, all important males had large tusks, and that was why the other humans were submissive, he said.

~~~~~~~~~~~~~~~~~~~~~~~~~~~~~

Shiro, being an animal of positive action, and not inclined to spend a lot of time mulling over things as that was simply a waste of time, decided she had to respond to Kolobe's ridiculous statement that she was "dense and not constipated".

How he could possibly know anything about her bodily functions was ludicrous. Unless someone had told the zebras, because she had a vague suspicion they weren't always completely loyal to her? And although she looked out for everyone at the zoo, and made sure to complain to those causing distress before chaos unfolded, she didn't always feel they appreciated her many efforts to keep everyone happy.

The monkeys were an example of this. On a few occasions, she'd had to send a message to them via the zebras, to tell the monkeys to be quiet and consider the other animals, especially the capybaras, who seemed quite excitable when other animals called out or moved quickly, and of course the zebras, who were very skittish too, with that foolish romping they did.

But there was the added difficulty of having to send her message via the zebras to the monkeys - the quickest route around the animal communication network. This entailed her having to be extra careful with her words, because she might need to mention the zebras' silliness to the monkeys, but she had to do this in a way which would not upset the zebras, who were her messengers.

Of course, she also had the option of sending her message the other way around the zoo, through most of the other animals, to the monkeys – a much longer route – but this was not very satisfactory, in her opinion. The replies to her messages always seemed a little garbled and not entirely relevant. She wondered if the other animals were deliberately distorting her words – sometimes they were disrespectful, so she wouldn't be entirely surprised by this.

As indeed was the case with Kolobe's nonsensical reply. What did he mean by "dense"? It didn't make sense.

Sometimes she was sure that the other animals had lost some of their brain power by being in this zoo. Perhaps it was due to them being caged and so close to each other?

But now she needed to reply to Kolobe, because there was nothing to be gained by thinking about how frivolous and irrational the other animals were.

~~~~~~~~~~~~~~~~~~~~~~~~~~~~~~~

12 – Separation Anxiety

A sad result of the little boy's antics at the elephant enclosure was that Ndlovu ended up being more enclosed.

The human workers had in the days following the unfortunate event, with a great deal of banging, knocking and shouting, placed tall metal poles and strong wire fencing all along the top of the elephant's walls, to ensure that no humans would ever be able to get up onto the walls again and almost fall into the depths below. And now, there was absolutely no chance they might be trampled by the elephant below.

Over time this had the effect of isolating Ndlovu the elephant even more than she had felt before. As you know, her large enclosure was purposefully dug down into the ground, and therefore the ground level of her cage was far below the ground level of the rest of the zoo, and was easily deeper than the height of an elephant.

Despite being a large animal, and thus having the advantage of tallness, Ndlovu simply couldn't see everything that went on in the zoo, as even when standing at the very back of her cage, she could only see some of the closer cages and animals, the heads and sometimes torsos of the human visitors who stared over her wall, the frequently overcast sky - and not much else.

Of course, the human zoo workers would come into her enclosure via a small door at the bottom of one side wall, to clean her space and freshen her food and water, more so on weekends before the human visitors arrived. So, although they got on with their chores and didn't interact much with her, she wasn't completely starved of company.

Ndlovu could also hear things that happened, and talk to the other animals via the animal communication network, which is how she maintained some contact with the outside world.

But nevertheless, the fence being added to the top of

her walls had the disheartening and detrimental effect of separating her from the others even more. She could still see their cages and the animals she had been able to see before: most often the parrots and Kolobe the warthog, every now and then some birds who flew freely outside of the cages, sometimes Noko the porcupine, and very occasionally, also Kulak the caracal.

But now most of the animals, through the wire of Ndlovu's newly added fencing, looked less clear or colourful than before, and sometimes they appeared to her to be just grey and blurry shapes moving about.

And so it was that Ndlovu would spend almost all her waking time partaking in a habit she had started before the added barrier, and one which gave her some comfort in her severely segregated situation.

More and more, she would stand in one spot of her enclosed pit, next to a dead tree, and sway backwards and forwards for hours.

Initially she pretended she was in the African landscape of her dreams and visions, with fellow elephants. She visualised walking freely and proudly as one of the herd, with her and the other elephants tugging leaves from the trees with their trunks, and pulling roots up in tufts from the ground to eat. Every now and then, as they walked and ate, the elephants would touch each other for reassurance with their trunks or bodies, and she felt secure knowing she was part of a caring and large herd.

She was aware of a warm and familiar wind across her shoulders and broad back, which sometimes blew her large ears outwards and made them flap. She could sense the grassy and dusty ground under her large, padded feet. It was warm too, and huge, grey, dusty spirals leapt up from it each time an elephant's foot plodded on the ground; it swept around in playful whirlwinds when she and the other elephants crossed an impossibly large plain; and it became redder in colour and more pliant, covering their toes, as they approached a muddy lake near some prickly trees.

She could smell the strong and sweet earthiness of the brown, muddy water on her back and head and squelching between her elephant toes, as she wallowed in the lake with the other elephants. She could see dust flying everywhere as the elephants, with their trunks, scooped it up and tossed swathes of it over their bodies to cool themselves; she closed her eyes momentarily as some soil hit her face and mingled with her tears, and then ran down her trunk to the ground from whence it came.

However increasingly Ndlovu wasn't able to go back to this beautiful, imaginary place, and simply bobbed side to side in her zoo enclosure without really knowing what she was doing or why.

It helped to pass the time, and enabled her to remove herself, at least in her mind, from the rambunctious human visitors and her feeling of forlorn separateness.

Once or twice though, she had been suddenly and rudely awoken from her distracted state. On one occasion, on a day when there weren't as many human visitors around, one of the human visitors had thrown a drinks can at her head.

Ndlovu had almost fallen over from the shock of being hit; the humans had laughed and run off before any others could catch them at it. The offending weapon had clattered to the ground and remained in her enclosure for another few days before one of the workers had collected it, after another human visitor had complained about the litter.

More recently a particularly large and noisy group of human visitors had gathered around the elephant pit. When they saw Ndlovu below, lost in her world and weaving to and fro, they had begun to shout and laugh and fall over each other, trying to get the best position to photograph and video the elephant with themselves in shot, proclaiming "the dumb elephant is playing with them".

Their loud frolics had disturbed her, and when she tried to retreat into her open shed behind the dead tree in her pit, they laughed some more.

KATHRYN ROSE NEWEY

13 – Fat in the Fire

Radati the rat quite enjoyed his stay at the little zoo, and his discussions with the zoo animals. He spent most of his time in Noko the porcupine's cage, eating Noko's food, drinking Noko's water, and curling up to sleep in the straw or in Noko's little box.

But of course Radati was at liberty to walk in and out

of any of the other animals' cages too, and use their beds or eat their food (although he drew the line at going into Kulak the caracal's cage – he wasn't a fool!).

During the talking sessions, Radati did most of the talking, while one or two of the other animals might occasionally make a comment, ask an incredulous question every now and then, or very infrequently even express doubt out aloud about what he said.

Radati was beginning to rather like these conferences, not only because the others seemed to look up to him in awe, but also because he was secretly entertained and amused by the other animals' complete ignorance of the real world.

Being as widely travelled as he was, he had seen and heard a lot of things. He knew, for instance, that the

THE ZOO ANIMALS' FARAWAY DREAM

way the animals in the little zoo were kept by humans in cages was not how it should be.

How did he know this?

Quite simply, because he and the other field and forest animals he had seen, were free and not in cages, and there was a sense of contentment and less anxiety about them.

He just knew it was better not to be locked in a cage - because he, himself, was free.

He noticed that the zoo animals didn't seem to behave like free animals. He watched how the zoo animals, some more than others, chewed their bars, looked at things but didn't really see them, or walked back and forth in their cages for hours; and he saw how they got confused and sad whenever they experienced the faraway dream.

On the other hand, the free animals seemed to simply get on with living: finding food, mating, building dens or nests, looking after their young, and sleeping. He had never heard of any free animals dreaming of other places and other times. It simply didn't happen.

Radati had told the zoo animals about those free animals of the fields and forests. And he seen how the zoo animals suffered from repeatedly dwelling on their faraway dreams, almost as if they were real.

In fact, Radati had a theory about it. He had seen the faraway dream become something that often destroyed the last bit of sanity of many of the caged animals he had visited in other places and this zoo.

And he had seen how the free animals were born, lived and died in the countryside surrounding the little zoo, as they were meant to, without humans.

~~~~~~~~~~~~~~~~~~~~~~~~~~~~~

The first time he had encountered caged animals was at a place not too far from this zoo. What he had seen had shocked him deeply. Before that, he hadn't known that some animals lived their whole lives in cages.

It had happened one day, soon after he had left the place in which he had been born. He had been following the delicious scent of some food he could smell a little further along, under a hedge. The aroma had driven him crazy – and he had rushed along, not really looking where he was going, lifting his nose and twitching his whiskers, being pulled along by all of the smell's promises and temptations.

Eventually he had found a box with some half-eaten

food, lying on its side, partly under the hedge - probably discarded by some humans as they leaned out of one of those huge, fast, noisy machines they always seemed to be travelling in.

Once he had eaten up all the tasty food and crumbs up (rats weren't fussy), he had burped loudly and sat up on his hind legs, just outside the hedge, cleaning his face and whiskers with his paws. Some sunshine had shone weakly in little patches, and he had to keep moving to catch it, before it disappeared again under those meddling clouds.

Although he had enjoyed eating the human food, he had to admit he hadn't felt very well afterwards. His stomach seemed to be making grumbling noises and he felt a little uncomfortable.

He was busy contemplating this, when another smell,

this time a very unpleasant and strong smell, penetrated his nostrils. He wrinkled his nose in disgust. It seemed to be coming from a very large building across a field in the distance.

It was then that he had begun to hear the noises too, wafting across on the wind. Moaning and whining and shrieking and crying.

Animals. Lots of them.

But Radati was pragmatic - he knew where there were buildings, there were humans, and where there were humans, there was food.

The noises of the crying animals and the stench was almost too much for him. Perhaps it was the thought of finding freely available food, or perhaps it was curiosity about the cries of the animals, but either way, Radati found himself moving determinedly towards the building.

~~~~~~~~~~~~~~~~~~~~~~~~~~~~

Shiro sent a very firm message to Kolobe.

It went via the animal communication network, starting with Noko, whose cage was next to the mongoose enclosure. She told Noko to pass this message to the other animals for Kolobe:

"Kolobe, I'm extremely disappointed that you're so obsessed with my ablutions – after all, that's private. What's more, there is nothing dense about me. Perhaps your brain isn't working anymore because you're too sceptical!"

Because she was a little cross when she related her message, she may have spoken rather quickly. And Noko, being a simple animal, didn't like to agitate Shiro further by asking her to repeat anything, so he simply reported the message, or as much as he could remember or had heard, to the parrots.

At the time, the parrots were having yet another argument about whether the faraway dream which some of them talked about so often now, was real or not. Of course, those who experienced it regularly were convinced it was a memory of real events, and were loud and increasingly vehement in insisting it was true.

They didn't like to admit that they couldn't explain how or why they could remember something which had nothing to do with being in a cage now. Some of the others, mostly the younger parrots who had been born to life in the zoo, screeched and squawked about how the older parrots were losing their minds and were not to be trusted with anything, anymore.

In fact, had the parrots not all been enclosed in close quarters with no possibility of escape, a coup by the younger parrots might have occurred.

As it was, the in-fighting meant that some parrots hunched miserably on the branch at the top of their cage, while others sulked defiantly on the ground below. Every now and then one of the ground-based parrots, tired of being on the floor, would flutter up - as best as he or she could with their clipped wings - and battle for a space amongst the branch-dwellers, who would peck and squeal at the unwelcome intrusion.

Hence Shiro's message was received and passed along in the midst of these hostile parrot skirmishes. One of the ground-based parrots happened to turn his back on the others, facing Noko's enclosure, and so heard Noko speaking. But what he heard and what he then repeated to the tortoise, who was housed next to the parrot cage, was in all likelihood already a different version to Shiro's original message.

~~~~~~~~~~~~~~~~~~~~~~~~~~~~

14 – Pig in a Poke

Ndlovu the elephant hadn't been the only animal to suffer renovations to her enclosure. After the penguins had been disturbed by the human night visitors, and the human workers had found the penguin cage decimated and some ruffled penguins wandering about the zoo aimlessly the next day, some repairs and reinforced fencing had been added to the penguin pond area.

The new fencing still allowed for human visitors to view the penguins in their enclosure, but it was now much more upright, slightly higher, more robust, and more resistant to movement should any humans lean on it, as they often did.

The penguins were now even more reserved than they had been before. No one knew exactly what they had suffered, that fateful night the human night visitors had come in and caused havoc, and the other animals didn't like to ask.

It frightened them all – they knew that the humans should not have been there, and they saw the effects of the incident in the way the penguins seemed to be confused afterwards, with a mixture of worried and blank expressions on their faces.

After the human night visitors had roughly torn down some of the penguin fencing, which had been frightening enough for the penguins, the humans had then chased and lunged at the penguins. One poor fellow, his feathers now more dishevelled than ever, had been picked up by the humans and thrown over the penguin enclosure fencing. He now walked with a permanent limp.

The penguins had been shocked to their core with this aggressive behaviour by the human night visitors.

They were used to the human workers coming into their enclosure to clean their pond area and fill their food bowls, but usually the human workers simply ignored the zoo animals while they did their jobs.

Once inside the enclosure with the penguins, the

human workers moved around with brooms or mops and buckets, and sometimes walked purposefully towards a corner where the penguins might be bunched up and trying to stay out of the way. The penguins would all rush over to another corner, squawking, and the human workers would continue doing their work.

It never took very long, because the human workers seemed to be in a rush and eager to get outside the animal enclosures, where they would all gather together, talking and laughing, for what seemed like most of the daylight hours to the animals.

But although the usual human workers might sometimes shout at the animals, and spent a lot of time ignoring them, they had never yet picked any animal up and thrown them.

Or certainly no animal had ever reported anything like that via the animal communication network.

~~~~~~~~~~~~~~~~~~~~~~~~~~~~~~

Long before Radati had reached the large building, the rowdy noises and pungent fumes were overwhelming.

But now he was more than curious; he had forgotten that he was investigating the availability of food, and needed to know what was causing those animals to cry and reek so terribly.

He ran along the edge of the building, using his whiskers and sense of smell to help find his way, but at the same time trying not to breathe in too much. He saw a small hole under the wall, where perhaps other rats had been, and entered the building.

It was dimly lit, so his eyes took some time to adjust.

THE ZOO ANIMALS' FARAWAY DREAM

By now, he was deliberately breathing through his mouth and not swallowing, because if he had breathed through his nose, he was sure he would have been sick.

In front of him were rows of cages with large openings between strong metal bars, stretching into the dim recesses of the inside of the building. It went on so far that he couldn't see an end. The dimness and stench seemed to mingle with each other, so that a dirty fog hung over everything. Here and there some lights blasted into the darkness, creating a bright circle around each light that was abrasive to the eyes.

Inside each of the open cages were some animals. They were large and fat animals, without fur but with coarse hairs, and with large snouts on the fronts of their faces.

Despite the gloominess, Radati could see they were very dirty and were so tightly packed into the metal cages that they couldn't help standing in their own waste – now he understood the horrible smell.

But as he stood and watched the strange scene before him, trying not to gag, he realised that the terrible smell was also one of fear, hopelessness, and desperation.

The animals looked at him but seemed to look through him. Some of those near to him tried to press back when he appeared, as if they thought he might strike at them. Some, perhaps lucky enough to be positioned to the front or sides of their dreadful enclosures, bit onto the metal bars repeatedly, as if they believed they could bite through them and escape.

The noise of gnawing, howling, snorting and screaming rose cacophonously and seemed to be coming from everywhere at once.

Radati was petrified. He whispered fearfully to an animal close to him "What is this place? What are you all doing here?"

Some of the nearby animals looked at him with interest, as if no one had ever asked them that question before, but they didn't answer. Their little eyes bore through him then clouded over, as if they couldn't or wouldn't see him. They were constantly busy with grunting and moaning and pushing and whimpering and chewing.

Radati turned and sprinted through the hole he had entered. He wanted to get away, as fast as he could, from this awful, disturbing place.

Once outside, with a slight breeze lifting the ghastly sounds and smells away, and the clouds rushing in to overshadow the truth, he tried to pretend that what he had just seen, heard and smelt wasn't real.

But as he ran away as fast as his legs could carry him, the pandemonium he had left behind felt like a wispy trail of miserable treachery following him and clinging to him.

~~~~~~~~~~~~~~~~~~~~~~~~~~~

15 – Calm Before the Storm

Once he had received it, Kolobe the warthog was astonished that Shiro the mongoose's message was so forthright.

He knew that Shiro was forceful, opinionated and bossy. Most of the animals in the little zoo had been, at one time or another, the target of her complaints or accusations. But nevertheless, some of the animals felt it was proper and right that Shiro voiced her concerns and kept everyone on their toes, claws or hooves, so to speak.

On the other hand, others didn't feel that one animal, and a small one at that, should tell them what to do and assert her views and opinions over the others. After all, they hadn't asked her to do it!

But mostly, no matter what they thought of her, the animals usually complied with Shiro's requests. It was easier to do what she asked, than to argue against her formidable will, or face her intimidating annoyance.

Shiro sensed that not everyone appreciated the enormous task she undertook – that of making sure that all the zoo animals were happy. She felt that she was doing a very good job, under the circumstances, and wished for a little more respect and gratitude, as well as unquestioning acquiescence. Her task wasn't easy, but it had to be done.

~~~~~~~~~~~~~~~~~~~~~~~~~~~~~

Kolobe noticed that lately his skin felt itchy all over. He scratched as best he could with his hooves, but his legs weren't particularly agile and didn't have a lot of reach. He whipped his tail onto his back, and this helped a little, but it wasn't very satisfactory. He rubbed his sides against the bars of his cage – but didn't notice that after a while, his skin was flaky and patchy, his coarse hairs were disappearing in places, and he had started to develop sores where he had scratched or rubbed himself raw.

It certainly wasn't the first time this had occurred.

He still remembered the last time, when after a lot of scratching and discomfort, eventually the human workers and a different human had come into his cage, and had grabbed him and pinned him down to the ground. As if that weren't humiliating and frightening enough, he had then felt a very painful stab on his rump before they had let him go. After that, his itchy skin had gradually got a little better, but now the troublesome and irritating affliction was back.

It didn't help that his snout, teeth and lips were painful and partly worn down too, and that eating was a little difficult for him these days. He was vaguely aware that this problem might have occurred because of his constant licking and attempted biting of the bars of his cage. But he simply couldn't stop – it was what he did, and it was an important activity every day, even though it was now more difficult to do.

He had noticed that the capybaras also seemed to be suffering when they tried to eat – they ate more slowly and sometimes couldn't eat for very long.

But Kolobe had seen that their teeth, instead of worn down like his, appeared to be quite long, and he wondered why. He was quite envious of their tusk-like teeth. Perhaps they were simpler creatures than him, and didn't need to partake in critical activities like biting or gnawing their cage bars?

Kolobe turned his thoughts once again to Shiro's message. He wondered why Shiro had suddenly become quite so radical. Her commanding and controlling nature was one thing. And being an animal who liked order himself, he felt that despite the unpleasantness of occasionally being dictated to by Shiro, he understood Shiro's attempts at keeping everyone in check.

But requiring the animals to rise up and protest was quite another matter altogether.

Shiro's surprising message to Kolobe, once it had come to him through the animal communication network - across walls, into and out of feeding troughs, over rocks, amongst hay and straw, around corners, up onto branches, down in the dust, and between bars, had eventually been:

"Kolobe, I'm appointing you to press for revolution. You need to riot, I implore. Arrange a defence campaign, stop shirking, and create a miracle!"

That Shiro had chosen him to play such a significant

role was appropriate, he felt. Kolobe was, after all, an animal who knew about structure and procedures. He was also, quite obviously, braver, more intelligent and better at making decisions than any of the others. So he wasn't surprised at all that she'd approached *him* for this important duty.

What was astounding about her message, after all her attempts to keep the animals calm and happy, was that it appeared she was now wanting him to incite some sort of animal rebellion.

Itchy skin and sore teeth aside, he knew instinctively that he was the animal for the job. He already possessed the stature, the dignity and the boldness required to get it done. Not to mention the most attractive tusks. And by choosing him, Shiro had somehow accurately noted in him a slightly defiant and independent nature too, which he felt was also an essential quality for this challenging role.

~~~~~~~~~~~~~~~~~~~~~~~~~~~~~

Radati knew he had to tell the zoo animals. Even for him, this was not something easy to do. But it had to be done.

And so he called them all together – Noko and the ones close by like the mongooses and parrots, and the ones further away like Kulak the caracal, who could just vaguely make out what he was saying if all was quiet, if he talked very loudly, and if she strained to hear him.

As for the rest, he knew that his message would eventually reach their ears via the animal communication network. Not that it was a completely adequate system of communicating, as Radati had already discovered.

THE ZOO ANIMALS' FARAWAY DREAM

On many occasions before, what he had said to Noko, the parrots, the mongooses and Kulak seemed to have been misrepresented, embellished or even exaggerated to the point they were nothing like his original statements.

He suspected that not all the animals fully understood his comments (after all, what he was saying about freedom was radical and implausible to those who had lived in cages for most of their lives), so perhaps his words were inadvertently, rather than deliberately, twisted?

But having made himself at home in Noko's cage, he did not particularly feel like disrupting his comfortable position, and so was not inclined to move around the zoo, repeating his speeches for the benefit of all the animals. Since they didn't always truly understand his reports anyway, he was not convinced that repeating these bulletins would necessarily change anything.

And so, from Noko's cage, he told them the distressing news once only, and let the animal communication network do the rest.

~~~~~~~~~~~~~~~~~~~~~~~~~~~

16 – A Moment of Truth

When he had been hurrying away from the huge building, so intent on getting away from its atrocities, Radati had almost bumped into a large bird with shiny, black feathers, who was pecking at something on the ground.

The bird had squawked and jumped away in fright, but then seemed to size Radati up, and must have come to the conclusion that he wasn't a threat, so hopped back to his snack.

Radati had been about to continue on his way, because he wanted to get as far away from the desperate howls and nauseating odours as possible. He couldn't seem to erase the image of all those dirty and distraught animals, trapped in such close quarters and living in such filthy and hopeless conditions, from his mind.

"Can't stand it then?" said the bird suddenly, in a unexpectedly rough voice. Radati jolted with surprise. He wasn't sure, but he thought he could hear the bird chuckling too.

He paused, then turned to face the bird.

"Er, no…it's just there's no food there…" he said, trying to sound as if he didn't care.

THE ZOO ANIMALS' FARAWAY DREAM

"You know what's going to happen to those animals?" asked the bird croakingly. He had the annoying habit of turning statements into questions.

Radati sat up, trying to look as if he were a rat of the world. Which he was, in a manner of speaking.

"Umm…" he said, trying to think of a clever way to answer.

"Isn't it a shame they're all going to be killed - and they don't know it?" wheezed the bird.

He pecked harder at the thing in the dust. Radati realised he was eating a flattened and very dead frog, which looked a little dry and not very appetising.

The bird looked up, and its round, bright eyes darted around, then bore into Radati, making him freeze on the spot.

"You know they keep them there for one thing only

– to make them fat so they can eat them?" he said, in a voice which was ragged, like he had talked too much – or, as Radati mused, perhaps because the bird had breathed in too much of that dreadful smell.

The bird was poking at his meal again, this time into what was once the frog's eye. By the time he looked up again, Radati had made a mad dash for the hedge and only some dust remained, marking his speedy path away from that place.

~~~~~~~~~~~~~~~~~~~~~~~~~~~~~

It was surprising to Kolobe how resistant the capybaras, monkeys and zebras were to his well thought-out scheme of active dissent. He had taken extra effort to painstakingly explain to the capybaras his fool-proof and excellent plan for the animals to all rise up and disobey, and how this would lead to the human workers letting them go free, eventually (he estimated it would take around two seasons).

Now freedom was something that all the animals thought about frequently and wished for, but in reality they were afraid of it.

It was a vague idea in their heads, and seemed to encompass something to do with being outside their cages, and the fields and forests and sunshine and winds of their faraway dreams.

It was also something that Radati the rat had described when he told them about the free animals who lived all around them, and whom they had never seen. Except for those free birds, of course, who flew and flittered and flapped just outside their cages.

They yearned deeply for it, their hearts sang from the

acute, blissful memories of it, and they truly immersed themselves in imagining the wonderfulness of living it.

But when they pulled themselves back from the brink of euphoria, they shrank in agitation and humiliation, fearful that there didn't seem to be any human workers in their dreams of freedom, and they worried about not getting fed, or not having cages to sleep in.

So when Kolobe had proudly and forcefully explained his plan of protest to them, the capybaras listened with wide eyes, then turned to each other and whispered about how Kolobe was suggesting something completely mad, how he wasn't a real leader, and how their current situation, in their cages and with human workers attending to them, was best.

The monkeys weren't much more enthusiastic. Kolobe felt they were quite hostile, in fact. They shrieked, hooted and babbled about how Kolobe's plan would never work and repeatedly questioned him in aggressive tones about how the human visitors would feed them human food, if somehow his plan worked and they ended up living outside their cages.

As for the zebras, well at least they got excited about it. When they heard of Kolobe's plan, they rushed around their cage, for once almost in synchronised movement, but when Mbizi, the youngest, shouted out in glee about her coming freedom, the usual chaos reigned and they all collided into each other, which resulted in Dube and Mbizi smashing so hard into their fence that they got cuts from it, and Goreb actually crashed to the ground.

From that moment on, Dube and Goreb were much more cautious, and on many occasions had to insist that Mbizi, who was still eager about the anarchistic plans, must stop obsessing about what they regarded as unrealistic fantasies of freedom.

In fact, when Kolobe thought about it, the tortoise was the most positive about his suggestions. Well, actually, all that he had received back from the tortoise was a resounding "yes". But it had made Kolobe feel appreciated for all the hard work he had undertaken in plotting the zoo animals' escape. Affirmative responses like that made it all worth it, and he was sure that Shiro the mongoose would be pleased with his vigorous efforts.

What Kolobe didn't know was that by the time his 'Great Escape' project had been conveyed around the animal communication network a few times, and had landed one morning in the tortoise's cage, via the garrulous parrots, the tortoise had simply heard that he should "wait for grapes".

~~~~~~~~~~~~~~~~~~~~~~~~~~~

But the various ways the animals reacted to Kolobe's call to action was very different to how they responded to what Radati eventually told them.

~~~~~~~~~~~~~~~~~~~~~~~~~~~

17 – Floods of Tears

It was raining again on the little zoo. Many of the animals curled up miserably in their boxes or sheds, trying to avoid the streams of water that somehow made their way into their cages and enclosures and brushed up against their fur and feathers, making them cold.

THE ZOO ANIMALS' FARAWAY DREAM

The rain, relentless in its efforts to dampen any enthusiasm or contentment the animals might feel, bore down on the cage roofs, sheds, enclosure walls and animals' backs.

And so it was even more difficult for the few animals closest to Noko's cage, to properly hear and understand Radati's last message.

Once the nearby animals were pressed against their cage walls and bars, as close to Noko's cage as they could bear without being physically absorbed into their cages, and with the rain coursing into their eyes and necks and ears, Radati began.

Even though he was an experienced orator, this time it was different. He shook his ears, licked his lips and looked up at the grey, wet sky, as if searching for inspiration for this important but final announcement.

Kulak the caracal watched him. In fact she had been watching him with great interest ever since he had arrived. She wasn't sure which animals evoked more excitement in her – the mongooses or the rat, but either way, gazing at them seemed to have the effect of making her feel hungry (even if she had just eaten).

Once when Radati had strayed out of Noko's cage, and was wandering along a passageway which the human visitors used on the days they came, Kulak had slowly stretched out one of her paws, reaching into the dust near him with her sharp claws braced, and had uttered a low, slow growl.

When Radati looked up in surprise, having been caught off guard for a second, Kulak had quickly withdrawn her paw back behind her bars and sat up, rhythmically licking her paws and cleaning behind her head and ears, as if nothing unusual had happened.

~~~~~~~~~~~~~~~~~~~~~~~~~~~~~

The rain, falling for so many days that it had forgotten how to stop, kept coming. There was so much of it that inevitably it got to the point where it had nowhere else to go, and started collecting where it fell.

Water came in everywhere. Nothing could escape it. It snaked under walls, through gaps no one knew were there. It pooled in depressions, causing miniature lakes, complete with little waves swelling and subsiding across the surfaces. It gushed in through larger holes meant for ventilation. It swayed and sashayed and spiralled around rocks, food bowls, walls, tree stumps and fences.

It gathered force and joined into larger streams, like liquid roads. It knocked small items over and lifted and carried them along with it, as if they were one with it. It lapped and gurgled at the animals' feet, and they splashed and sloshed through it, panicking, trying desperately to get away, somehow knowing that water in this quantity was perilous.

But they were trapped. Trapped in their cages and enclosures which had held them captive for as long as they could remember.

Some could climb or cling frantically and perilously onto higher items such as rocks, trees, sleeping boxes, branches or sheds.

But others could not.

The zebras, with only a shed to one side which offered some shelter from the elements at other times, were not climbing animals. They whinnied and snorted in panic and terror, and trampled each other, trying to run and jump out of the rising water.

The tortoise, ordinarily a slow and ponderous animal, tried to walk away from the water. His clawed feet moved continuously, making walking motions, but the water lapped at his shell, curled in under it, seeped in under his neck skin and threatened to lift him up in its swirls. The force of the current pushed him this way and that, and had he been just a little lighter, perhaps it would have lifted him up. Instead he soon found he was walking under water, and when his neck could no longer stretch up to keep his head above the water, his nostrils filled with it.

~~~~~~~~~~~~~~~~~~~~~~~~~~~~~

Radati's theory was simply this: he had come to believe that the faraway dreams so many of the caged animals occupied their time with, were indeed memories of times they had been free. Before the humans had caught them and put them into cages.

And so he began his speech. He described to the zoo animals the large building he had seen on that harrowing day in the distant past. He told them about the trapped, stinking animals inside the building, also in cages, who had kept calling out for help but none had come. Then he paused.

He knew what he had to tell them next would not be easy for the zoo animals to hear. And he knew that as soon as he had said it, he would have to leave the little zoo.

THE ZOO ANIMALS' FARAWAY DREAM

~~~~~~~~~~~~~~~~~~~~~~~~~~~~~~~

The rain, never one to sense when enough was enough, simply kept falling. It dropped out of the sky as if it was in a hurry to reach the ground, and when it hit the earth, it flew up in angry splashes. Then it spouted through holes too narrow for animals to squeeze through, and cascaded into hollows made by sleepy animals in dryer times. It crept like small tides across puddles, and lapped majestically at walls, knowing it was only a matter of time before it reached around, over or under them.

The mongooses, crying out in shrill, panicky voices, were trying to stay aloft their rock pile to escape the rising waters, but there were too many of them, and the unlucky, outermost animals kept falling down into the water. At first it didn't matter too much; the water made only muddy puddles in the deeper parts of their dens.

But the rain was single-minded and vengeful; it surged around the mongoose enclosure, gathering momentum, then started accumulating and ascending up the walls and the rock pile that so far had kept the mongooses safe from its destructive intentions.

~~~~~~~~~~~~~~~~~~~~~~~~~~~~~~

18 – Still Waters Run Deep (Ending One)

Radati decided the best way forward was to just say it. There was no hiding the truth. He sighed, then took a deep breath.

"Like those animals in the big building I saw, I'm sorry to tell you, but you…"

Noko the porcupine had looked at him searchingly, and Radati had hesitated for a moment. But it had to be said.

"You are in cages because the humans want to kill you and eat you", he finished, speaking rather hurriedly and breathlessly, and a little less arrogantly than usual.

Then he looked away, a little sadly, remembering those poor, large, trapped animals in the big building which he had seen a while ago, and which the bird outside the building had enlightened him about.

The zoo animals weren't quite sure they'd heard Radati correctly. What he was claiming was astounding and unbelievable.

And yet, Radati had claimed outlandish things before, such as the free animals he told them about who he claimed lived in the outside world, without needing humans. There was some evidence for this – all the zoo animals had witnessed birds living freely outside cages.

The animals looked at each other, too fearful to speak, the coldness of the rain gripping their hearts, and their minds racing with all sorts of questions. Could what Radati was now saying be true?

Despite fearing freedom, they had to admit, perhaps quietly to themselves, that they craved freedom almost as much as they needed food, water and sleep. So why then did the humans keep them in cages?

Noko the porcupine, up to his ankles in water, suddenly broke the silence. He hadn't been a fan of Kolobe's breakout plan, when he had first heard about it via the animal communication network.

In fact, he was not even sure he had heard it correctly, because the idea of animals leaving the zoo was revolutionary and unheard of. And he, like many other animals, had been worried about how they would survive outside their enclosures and without humans, should the ground-breaking plans become real.

But now it suddenly felt to him like the right time. He felt a new sense of purpose in his porcupine heart, and knew, without a shadow of a doubt, that escaping the zoo was something all the animals must embrace and carry out, urgently.

"We must go now!" Noko exclaimed, sounding more confident than he felt.

But it wasn't clear as to whether anybody had

actually heard him, and when he looked around, seeking Radati's approval, the rat was nowhere to be seen.

~~~~~~~~~~~~~~~~~~~~~~~~~~~~

The rain, now sure it had the upper hand, and having blocked the sun out for days, slowed for a few hours and then stopped, having simply exhausted itself. The clouds which had taken over the sky pulled back in places, and even permitted the sun to peek through for short moments.

But the rain's abatement happened too late for some of the zoo's animals.

By the time the human workers had waded into the zoo wearing rubber boots and waterproof clothing, and had organised themselves with ropes and carry-boxes and temporary enclosures, breaking open the cages and hauling animals out, some of the animals had perished, the water having risen too high and having engulfed them.

The ones that were still alive resisted being rescued by the humans, kicking and clawing and screaming wildly as much as they could.

Radati's final and terrible warning rang through their minds, even though they hadn't completely believed him at the time. They fought being saved by the humans, not knowing what was happening or where they would be taken to. They didn't want to be killed and eaten, like the dirty and troubled, confined animals Radati had described from before.

~~~~~~~~~~~~~~~~~~~~~~~~~~~~~

The little zoo was an unhappy place.

It took some time for the flood waters to subside

and for the human workers to find and rescue the animals who had survived.

They left the larger animals like Ndlovu the elephant, the zebras, the monkeys and Kulak the caracal in their watery, muddy and smelly enclosures. These animals were still alive only by virtue of being taller, or being able to climb, and thus had been able to keep their heads above the flood waters when they were at their highest.

Bus alas, when the humans searched some of the smaller animal cages, they found the slumped, icy cold bodies of animals who had tried everything to escape the waters but had been held in by their cages, and who had gulped their last breaths looking out of their bars and walls at unattainable freedom.

The clouds, feeling a little remorseful, disappeared

for a few days and allowed the sun to attempt the impossible task of drying out the earth below it. Some thin, sickly stripes of sunlight reached hesitantly into the little zoo's cages, but recoiled when they realised everything was covered in swirled, brown, rotting mud – the food bowls, the sleeping boxes, the hay and straw, and the animals' lifeless bodies.

~~~~~~~~~~~~~~~~~~~~~~~~~~~~~~

And so it was that the little zoo, after a brief period of closure for 'cleaning operations', had opened its doors to the public again.

The unfortunate event had only served to make it more popular – human visitors flocked to see it, to wonder at the horror of the flood, and to gawk at the animals who had survived.

THE ZOO ANIMALS' FARAWAY DREAM

Although some cages remained sealed off and closed to the public, others had been restocked with new mongooses, reptiles and other species. There were no longer capybaras or a warthog, but the zoo's main attraction, Ndlovu the elephant, was still popular with the human visitors, who liked to film themselves with her in the background, claiming they and the elephant were "survivors, LOL."

Ndlovu, now even more immune to this attention from the humans than before, simply swayed and bobbed for hours.

Perhaps she didn't see them or hear them, couldn't see them or hear them, or maybe she no longer cared whether she could see or hear anything at all.

~~~ The End (Ending One) ~~~

~~~~~~~~~~~~~~~~~~~~~~~~~~~~

~~~~~~~~~~~~~~~~~~~~~~~~~~~~~

Sadly, the previous ending (Ending One) is a likely and realistic scenario for lots of zoos around the world.

~~~~~~~~~~~~~~~~~~~~~~~~~~~~~

I invite you to consider another possibility.

For a different ending (Ending Two), we'll now re-join the story from the end of Chapter 17.

Keep reading…

~~~~~~~~~~~~~~~~~~~~~~~~~~~~~

THE ZOO ANIMALS' FARAWAY DREAM

18 – Still Waters Run Deep (Ending Two)

Those animals who thought they'd heard Radati correctly shook their heads sadly.

If he'd said what they thought he'd said, it simply couldn't be true. Could it?

Noko the porcupine was the most shocked. He was an animal who felt that things in this world were either one way or another way, and not anything in between. As far as he was concerned, things that Radati had said before had seemed to be true. Noko couldn't believe that anyone would lie. Even if they did, he was too polite to say so, so it was easier for him to assume everyone told the truth.

But now he found himself in the unusual position of wondering if this latest statement of Radati's was true, and even considering the unlikely and much more complicated possibility that Radati might not be speaking the truth, although Noko couldn't explain why.

Radati had claimed that all the zoo animals were kept in cages by the human workers, because the humans (and Noko trembled at the very thought of this) were going to kill the animals and eat them. Just like what would happen to all those other terrified, stinky, overcrowded animals in the large building Radati had told them about before.

Noko sank slowly to the floor of his cage and lay there, staring at the familiar corners and his weathered box, and the dirty leaves, dust and bits of food, now mingling with mud and swirls of water.

~~~~~~~~~~~~~~~~~~~~~~~~~~~~

The mongooses, pressed tightly against their enclosure wall, chattered in fear when they heard it. Some of the teenage girls started wailing, and some of the younger ones ran round and round in helpless circles.

One of the older mongooses, old enough to remember Mungo and his botched attempts at escaping the enclosure, started climbing the pile of rocks and sand, determined to escape, even though

Mungo, and other mongooses after him, had never succeeded.

Shiro decided to take control.

"That's utter nonsense" she said, shouting to get their attention.

"Why would the humans feed us and look after us, if they were simply going to eat us?"

Her logic made absolute sense to her.

Some of the mongooses stopped moaning, realising that Shiro might have a point, for once.

The zebras, as you might have expected, hadn't been quite so sensible. On hearing the terrible news, Mbizi had galloped full tilt into their fence and collapsed to the ground in despair.

Goreb and Dube had tried to console her, talking to

her about the faded picture of wide, grassy plains stuck to the outer wall of their cage. Eventually Mbizi had quietened, but she'd stayed where she'd fallen; she no longer felt the need to get up onto her feet.

~~~~~~~~~~~~~~~~~~~~~~~~~~~~~

And so, as the rain began to fall harder and with more resolve, filling holes, channels and pathways with cold doggedness mixed with the malice of the grey, grim clouds, many of the animals, now defeated, simply didn't bother to seek shelter in their misshapen and dirty sleeping boxes and sheds.

The rain, gushing incessantly for days, had created a world full of water, or so it had seemed to the caged and miserable zoo animals. Their unhappiness and the cold, unfriendly rain seemed to fuse; it felt like even their souls were flooded. They had stood, bunched miserably and with heads down, water running into their eyes and ears, fur and feathers, their tears mixing with the torrents from the sky.

When the humans had come, finally realising that the relentless rain meant the animals were in danger, the animals had fought and cried and kicked, Radati's final words ricocheting in their heads.

~~~~~~~~~~~~~~~~~~~~~~~~~~~~

Ndlovu tried to ignore it. She was good at shutting out the other animals, the human visitors and workers, but she couldn't see where she was going. They'd shoved her and pulled her, putting chains around her feet and belly, and hauled her up a ramp into some kind of enclosed container.

It was dark, so she'd pretended she was in her shed

at the zoo, imagining the night sky above her, consoled by its twinkling stars and fiercely bright, round moon, which always seemed friendlier than the weaker sliver of a moon, playing hide and seek behind some wispy, lonely night time clouds.

But the shouts of human workers, and the thuds and clangs as they shut her into the container, made worse by a constant, loud roaring sound, had unnerved her.

She'd started shaking.

Even if Radati was right, and she was about to die, she simply felt numb. Like it didn't matter, one way or the other.

She shuddered, reaching out with her trunk to steady herself, as the container seemed to be moving, and she kept falling one way or the other.

~~~~~~~~~~~~~~~~~~~~~~~~~~~~~~

The roaring stopped. Some humans shouted, there was a bang, then light streamed into the box.

Kolobe the warthog sniffed.

Everything was quiet.

He gingerly stretched out a back leg, and his hoof felt air. He reversed out some more.

The sounds of birds tweeting, singing and cooing - the sounds free birds made - reached his ears and he shook his head, to be sure.

He could smell the humans, and hear some soft talking and laughing, but they weren't near.

He decided to run for it.

~~~~~~~~~~~~~~~~~~~~~~~~~~~~~~

Ndlovu couldn't believe her eyes.

THE ZOO ANIMALS' FARAWAY DREAM

In front of her was a grassy pasture. Trees and bushes grew in clumps and she could see a row of trees, far in the distance, which shimmered, seeming to join the ground to the sky.

She inched forward.

The container creaked.

She could feel a light breeze coaxing her out. It wasn't the warm, intense breeze of her dreams, but it carried a faint promise of something gentle and hopeful.

She took another step, stopping to breathe in the pungent earthiness of life all around her which streamed into her trunk.

As she reached the bottom of the ramp, her toes touched the ground. In that moment, it was as if she'd been connected to something bigger than herself, and the excitement of being alive jolted her awake.

She gave a little squeal of joy and started running across the grass.

~~~~~~~~~~~~~~~~~~~~~~~~~~~~~

And so it was that Kolobe the warthog, the three zebras, Noku the porcupine and Ndlovu the elephant shared a large paddock with two other rescued elephants, five gazelles, and a tall, grey bird with a broken wing called Greta.

Most of the little zoo's other animals had also been rescued - even the tortoise had been snatched out of the flood waters a moment before he'd succumbed to the water filling his nostrils - and they now lived in larger, more comfortable enclosures, with plenty of bushes, branches, shelters and even toys, or in fields like the one Ndlovu was to spend the rest of her life in, filled with tasty plants and shady trees, and away from crowds of human visitors.

Even Shiro the mongoose, older and slower these days, spent more time warming her greying fur in the sun when it shone, or under a special mongoose heater when it didn't, in a much larger mongoose enclosure, while the younger mongooses played and dug happily amongst the ample sandy burrows, tunnels, rocks and bushes, which seemed just like the place of their faraway dreams.

~~~ The End (Ending Two) ~~~

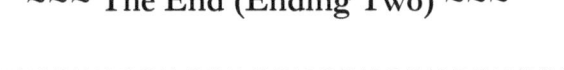

~ *This is the End of the Story with two Endings, but not of the Book* ~

Read the next few chapters in Part Two to explore facts and information about zoo animals and other confined animals - with website links to research the issues further.

And, most importantly, find out how you can help save caged animals.

PART TWO ~ THE TRUTH

KATHRYN ROSE NEWEY

THE ZOO ANIMALS' FARAWAY DREAM

19 – About Caged Animals

I would like to put the following ideas to you for your consideration:

- It is never 'good', 'kind' or 'normal' to keep animals in captivity, no matter how 'natural', 'large' or 'clean' their cages/tanks/enclosures appear, or how 'nice' or 'caring' their human keepers seem.

- Animals confined in cages, tanks, enclosures or chains in zoos, circuses, aquatic/water parks and roadside zoos/farms are simply prisoners!

- Think about it. If animals are kept in captivity, they have been restricted from normal, free lives and have been reduced to imprisoned slaves, for the purposes of entertaining or serving humans.

Read on to find out why I say this, and to learn more about animals kept in confinement...

~~~~~~~~~~~~~~~~~~~~~~~~~~~~~

Facts about caged and confined animals

Being kept in cages or cramped, unnatural quarters and sometimes being made to perform tricks means animals are often traumatized, bored, lonely and unhealthy.

It's very common for animals to suffer from distress, depression and dysfunctional behaviour (such as constant swaying, head bobbing, pacing, chewing, or other repetitive behaviour, referred to as 'zoochosis' or 'stereotypy' – a form of mental illness) as a result of being cramped, unstimulated, and separated from family or pack members.

Confined animals are not able to behave normally and often cannot properly or fully move, feed, play, socialize and mate as they need to do. Many animals in captivity, especially larger and more intelligent animals, tend to live unnaturally short lives – they often suffer from illnesses and disease and die much earlier, compared to those living in the wild.

In order to obtain animals for zoos, circuses and

shows, sometimes baby animals are stolen from their mothers in the wild (whilst their family members are killed in front of them), and in many cases the baby animals are then repeatedly abused, beaten, prodded, shouted at, chained and starved in order to 'break' their spirits and make them submissive to their human keepers or trainers. All in order to 'train' them to be tame, meek and/or to routinely perform meaningless and unnatural tricks for paying human visitors. For example, did you know that over 70% of elephants in European zoos today were wild-caught?

~~~~~~~~~~~~~~~~~~~~~~~~~~~~~

Read on for some information and websites which explore these issues further, and to find out more about zoos…

THE ZOO ANIMALS' FARAWAY DREAM

See these websites for more information

People for the Ethical Treatment of Animals (PETA) discuss '8 Facts About Animals in Captivity' which will change the way you think about animals in captivity: *https://www.peta2.com/news/captive-animal-facts/* [or search online for: PETA 8 facts animals in captivity]

Freedom for Animals explains why zoos fail animals in their article '10 Facts About Zoos': *https://www.freedomforanimals.org.uk/Blog/10-facts-about-zoos* [or search online for: freedom for animals 10 facts about zoos]

This article discusses scientific findings of zoo monkeys showing additional stress from being stared at by human visitors. It argues that many animals feel threatened when being stared at directly, and so humans constantly looking into cages at animals can result in zoo animals becoming anxious or aggressive:

http://www.onegreenplanet.org/animalsandnature/how-monkeys-really-feel-about-living-in-captivity/ [or search online for: onegreenplanet how monkeys really feel about living in captivity]

One Green Planet discusses the differences between captive and wild animals:

http://www.onegreenplanet.org/animalsandnature/the-life-of-animals-in-captivity-versus-the-wild/ [or search online for: onegreenplanet animals in captivity versus the wild]

This article in the Guardian lists many recent cases of baby and young elephants being legally taken from the wild and sold to zoos around the world, including zoos in China, Europe and the USA:

https://www.theguardian.com/environment/2017/apr/06/

THE ZOO ANIMALS' FARAWAY DREAM

secret-footage-obtained-of-the-wild-elephants-sold-into-captivity-in-chinese-zoos [or search online for: guardian secret footage of wild elephants sold in captivity for chinese zoos]

~~~~~~~~~~~~~~~~~~~~~~~~~~~~~~

Read on to find out how we came to have zoos in the world...

20 – About Zoos

History of zoos

The first zoos were collections of animals (menageries) created and kept by royals, wealthy people and those in power, probably to show off!

Eventually zoos became places where the general

public could come and wonder at creatures from continents far away, which they would probably never be able to view in the wild during their lifetimes.

Gradually the larger zoos became more aware of animal behaviour and the distress animals felt when confined in cages and enclosures, so many of the more famous zoos in the world now have bigger and more natural enclosures for their animals, and stricter rules on how they look after their animals, as well as how they obtain animals.

However zoo animals are still not free to act normally, no matter how 'natural' their enclosures and diets are, and how caring their keepers are. Studies have shown that animals in zoos live in thousands of times less space than what they would typically need and have if living in the wild.

Unfortunately around the world there are still plenty of smaller zoos, roadside zoos, circuses and places where animals are kept tied or chained up, or in impossibly small cages or tanks for their whole lives, sometimes made to perform tricks or work for humans, often without proper food or medical care, in dirty conditions, and in sad, distressed and mentally-ill states.

Find out more: *https://en.wikipedia.org/wiki/Zoo* [or search online for: wikipedia zoo]

~~~~~~~~~~~~~~~~~~~~~~~~~~~

Read on to find out why we still have lots of zoos in the world...

THE ZOO ANIMALS' FARAWAY DREAM

If zoos aren't good, why do we have them?

In my opinion, there are three main reasons why we still have zoos, despite the fact that many people now know and understand how animals suffer in captivity.

The first reason is historical – public zoos were started in the 1800's and many of those zoos are still open nowadays. They can't simply close, because the bigger zoos earn lots of money and are profitable corporations before anything else. Also, they wouldn't necessarily be able to find suitable homes for all their animals if they did close.

The second reason is that zoos claim to fulfil an educational function. Like the zoos of long ago, people often visit zoos to marvel at and sometimes learn about animals from all over the world, many of which they feel they might never be able to see in the wild.

The third reason has to do with science and conservation. Some people, often the owners or shareholders of some zoos, wildlife parks, circuses, water parks and so forth, claim that keeping animals captive helps to serve nature conservation. The argument goes that some endangered species or even animals that are extinct in the wild have been bred in captivity and thus saved from extinction. Scientists claim that animals in captivity can be more easily studied. Some people also claim that some zoo animals are only kept in captivity temporarily until they can be released back into the wild.

See more about the debate at:
https://www.theatlantic.com/news/archive/2016/06/harambe-zoo/485084/ [or search online for: why do we

have zoos]

~~~~~~~~~~~~~~~~~~~~~~~~~~~~~

Read on to see why not all of these pro-zoo claims are completely true…

KATHRYN ROSE NEWEY

Zoos: the whole truth

Some captive species may indeed have been saved from extinction by zoos, and in certain cases animals are released back into the wild. But generally captive animals cannot be released, because they don't have the skills to survive in the wild, and if released they will also need to be protected from poaching and habitat loss, or they won't thrive or necessarily stay alive if released.

It's worth noting that most animals in captivity around the world are not endangered; captive animals often don't breed as successfully as wild animals, but when they do, the resulting offspring are often sent to other zoos, not back into the wild, or are culled (killed); and almost all animals in captivity will suffer from the various problems related to being confined, regardless of the reasons for being held captive.

And perhaps we ought to consider, like the following article argues: if zoos save animal species, but then humans can only view those animals in captivity, behaving abnormally, rather than in the wild where they're meant to roam free - is this really what we humans should be encouraging and partaking in?

See this website:

http://www.onegreenplanet.org/animalsandnature/zoos-bringing-endangered-species-back-from-the-brink/ [or search online for: onegreenplanet zoos bringing endangered species back from the brink]

~~~~~~~~~~~~~~~~~~~~~~~~~~~~~

Read on for what the solutions could be...

KATHRYN ROSE NEWEY

Shouldn't we let all caged animals go free?

I'm not claiming that the tragic issue of caged and confined animals is an easy one to solve.

In reality wild animals already living in, or released into, natural and wild environments are at a huge risk from decreasing habitats due to human developments, diminishing food supplies and competition with humans for food and space, theft for wildlife trafficking, as well as hunting and poaching (being killed for body parts or meat).

So at the moment, unfortunately we cannot simply let all zoo animals free into the wild, as much as we might hope for their freedom! But there's plenty we can do to help.

The solution needs to be a combination of responding to and solving all the issues that cause animals to be held captive and/or stolen from the wild in the first place, as well as ensuring that wild animals, and those placed back in the wild, can live freely without human competition, interference, theft and poaching.

We need to start now. There are lots of professionals and ordinary people already involved in this process, but the first step for anyone (like you and me) is to at least become aware of these issues. This will mean we can help make other people aware, and then all make more informed decisions about our actions to help, rather than harm animals.

I'd also like to acknowledge and express gratitude to those people and organisations who are trying through numerous ways to solve or reduce the many and complicated problems of animals in captivity, animal abuse and cruelty, animal trafficking, wild animal hunting and poaching, and habitat loss.

~~~~~~~~~~~~~~~~~~~~~~~~~~~~

See Chapter 21 for some suggestions on how you can help…

21 – *How Can You Help?*

There are lots of things you can actively do, or actions you should avoid, which will either help captive animals have better quality lives, or help work towards their freedom from captivity. Here are some suggestions:

- Become aware of all the issues surrounding

captive and caged animals, and do your best to educate others about this issue.

- Don't support or attend places that keep animals captive – even if they claim or seem to keep animals in 'humane' conditions. Stay away from zoos, circuses, wildlife parks and aquatic/water parks – in fact, anywhere where animals are kept in unnatural conditions. It's better to see animals living freely in the wild, for example in game reserves, or in wild animal rescue sanctuaries - the latter two types of places need your support, to ensure they are able to afford continued provision of safe and more natural homes for wild animals.

- Don't pay for or partake in any activities where captive animals are kept to entertain or serve humans, such as circuses, elephant rides, donkey rides, horse and carriage rides, bullfights, swimming with dolphins, horse/greyhound racing, or having your photograph taken with a wild animal. Paying for or partaking in these types of activities encourages people to offer these in exchange for money, and in many cases their animals might not be looked after properly, suffer from stress and exhaustion due to being forced to work continuously, and may have been stolen from the wild initially.

- Don't buy souvenirs which look as if they may contain animal parts (such as ivory or fur), even if sellers or shops claim they don't, and don't eat 'venison'/'wild steaks'/'bushmeat', etc, as animals may have been cruelly or illegally trapped and killed for this meat.

- Remember that even those people who

claim they have a right to confine or hurt animals 'because it's their culture', simply do NOT have any excuse or justification to cage or abuse animals. Animals are sentient beings, just like you and me, and deserve as much chance to live and thrive on this Earth without interference, cruelty or enslavement.

This website lists ways you can consider and help animals when travelling/holidaying (applicable to any visits to animal parks/zoos):

https://www.worldanimalprotection.org.uk/protect-animals/our-guide-to-animal-friendly-travel [or search online for: WAP guide to animal friendly travel]

~~~~~~~~~~~~~~~~~~~~~~~~~~~~~

THE ZOO ANIMALS' FARAWAY DREAM

~~~~~~~~~~~~~~~~~~~~~~~~~~~

Finally, see Chapter 22 for important facts and statistics about zoos and animals held captive in places other than zoos, the groups trying to help them, and website links to find out more…

~~~~~~~~~~~~~~~~~~~~~~~~~~~

22 – *More Things to Know*

Sadly millions of animals are held captive all their lives, some having been stolen from the wild initially - all in order to serve, feed, or entertain humans, usually for profit.

Here are some more websites with information about caged/confined animals and some organisations trying to help:

Culling of zoo animals

One of the saddest things about zoos is that they often end up with 'surplus' animals, either through breeding, disease or lack of space – and so they cull them or have them 'put down' (kill them): *http://www.bbc.co.uk/news/magazine-26356099* [or search online for: bbc how many healthy animals do zoos put down]

Factory farming

ADAPTT's "The Kill Counter" shows a continuous count of how many animals are killed by the meat, egg and dairy industries, since the moment you open their webpage (150 Billion animals every year). Many of these animals are confined in tiny enclosures all their lives on factory farms, then cruelly killed in horrific, but so-called 'humane' slaughterhouses: *http://www.adaptt.org/about/the-kill-counter.html* [or search online for: ADAPTT kill counter]

Collective Evolution's facts about factory farmed animals explains how factory farms keep farm animals in small cages or cramped conditions for their whole lives, and feed them a combination of food and chemicals to make them grow faster or give more milk/eggs. This is the method used to rear most farm animals for meat, milk, leather and wool in the world (2 out of every 3 farm animals). Note that although the statistics quoted are from the USA, factory farming is very common in many countries of the world, including the UK, Canada, Australia, New Zealand and Europe: *http://www.collective-evolution.com/2014/03/21/10-alarming-facts-about-factory-farms-that-will-break-your-heart/* [or search online for: 10 alarming facts about factory farms]

Organic Consumers Association's article talks about some of the awful substances factory-farmed animals are regularly fed:

https://www.organicconsumers.org/news/they-eat-what-what-are-they-feeding-animals-factory-farms [or search online for: what are they feeding animals on factory farms]

Fur farming

Fur Free Alliance (FFA) describes how each year 100 Million animals are cruelly confined and killed for their fur: *https://www.furfreealliance.com/fur-farming/* [or search online for: FFA fur farming]

This newspaper report in the Independent exposes UK companies who sell items with fake fur, which is actually made from real animal fur (December 2017): *http://www.independent.co.uk/news/uk/home-news/uk-*

retailers-selling-fur-faux-fox-rabbit-shoes-coat-amazon-groupon-boohoo-tk-maxx-a8121241.html [or search online for: independent major retailers selling real animal fur]

Laboratory animals / animal experiments

Over 100 Million animals, including mice, rats, dogs, cats, birds, monkeys, guinea pigs and rabbits, are confined and used or killed in animal testing and experiments (vivisection) every year. This is despite the fact that often the tests are no longer required, tests on animals do not show safety of products/chemicals for humans, and unimaginable cruelty against these confined animals is allowed which would be considered illegal crimes in any other context: *https://www.dosomething.org/us/facts/11-facts-about-animal-testing* [or search online for: facts about animal testing]

Sourcing zoo animals

Even in 2018, many zoo animals are still captured in the wild, often as babies, and forced to live for the rest of their lives confined in zoos. For example, Network For Animals (NFA) have been working to free 31 baby elephants abducted from the wild in Zimbabwe and shipped to zoos in China (January 2018): *https://networkforanimals.org/petitions/petition-to-investigate-the-recent-export-of-31-baby-elephants-to-china/* [or search online for: NFA petition on export of 31 baby elephants]

War and zoo animals

Zoo animals are often forgotten when war comes. Four Paws animal charity rescued the last few remaining animals abandoned in a zoo in war-torn Aleppo, Syria (2017). Most of the zoo's other 150 animals died from bombs, stress or starvation: *http://www.vier-pfoten.org/en/projects/emergency-response-and-disaster-relief/rapid-response-in-syria/* [or search online for: four paws rescue aleppo zoo animals]

Waterparks and aquariums

It is documented and well-known that many of the world's waterparks, dolphinariums and aquariums choose and capture the dolphins for their parks/shows at Japan's annual 'Taiji kill'. The Dolphin Project has written 'Taiji Facts/FAQs' which covers everything you need to know about the horrific annual slaughter and capture of hundreds of dolphins in Taiji, Japan (this still happens, even in 2018).

These captured dolphins, who will be trained to do tricks in shows for paying humans all over the world, will have witnessed their family members being trapped and slaughtered in front of them, before they are hauled off to a life in confinement: *https://dolphinproject.com/campaigns/save-japan-dolphins/frequently-asked-questions/* [or search online for dolphin taiji facts]

~~~~~~~~~~~~~~~~~~~~~~~~~~~~

To all caged and confined animals worldwide:

May humans see,

One day set you free,

And let you be.

Love and strength.

~~~~~~~~~~~~~~~~~~~~~~~~~~~~

KATHRYN ROSE NEWEY

THE ZOO ANIMALS' FARAWAY DREAM

~~~~~~~~~~~~~~~~~~~~~~~~~~~~~

If you enjoyed reading this book or were moved by it, **please consider leaving a review** *at amazon or the website you purchased it, or by contacting the author at* **KathrynRoseNewey.com.** *Alternatively, you could visit her Facebook Page at www.facebook.com/KathrynRoseNeweyAuthor to leave a review there.*

By writing a review, you are supporting the author and helping other readers. Thank you.

~~~~~~~~~~~~~~~~~~~~~~~~~~~~~

KATHRYN ROSE NEWEY

About the Author

Kathryn Rose Newey is a teens' and children's book writer, poet and environmental author. She is passionate about ordinary people helping to solve the world's environmental and animal crises.

Her first book, **Animals in the Forest: The Day Terrible Things Came**, *is told from the point of view of wild animals, who become distressed and confused when their peaceful existence is placed in jeopardy by human activity in their forest. But it's more than just an animal story. As the story unfolds, it highlights environmental issues which children, parents, carers, teachers and home-schoolers may wish to think about, discuss, explore further and act on.*

The book also honours young environmental activists, defenders, protectors, indigenous tribes and places where ordinary people like you and me stood up for their rights to land, air and water. These are listed at the back of the book, as are websites for more information.

As a further aid to learning and growing, a complete booklet of supplementary literacy and environmental WonderWorksheets is also available to support readers.

Visit the author's website to find out more:
KathrynRoseNewey.com

www.ingramcontent.com/pod-product-compliance
Lightning Source LLC
LaVergne TN
LVHW021702060526
838200LV00050B/2471